P9-CRK-162

Courtney
1986

Changes
the Game

by Kellen Hertz

★ American Girl®

Rockport Public Library
17 School Street
Rockport MA 01966

A PEEK INTO

Courtney's World

Orange Valley Mall is totally tubular! Courtney loves playing video games at the arcade and hanging out with her friends.

Courtney's Family and Friends

Mom
Courtney's mom, who is running for mayor

Mike
Courtney's stepdad, who owns an electronics store in the mall

Dad
Courtney's dad, a software engineer

Tina
Courtney's 13-year-old stepsister

Rafi
Courtney's and Tina's two-year-old half brother

Kip Tomatsu
Courtney's
gamer friend

Sarah Barrett
Courtney's outspoken
best friend

Justin Wilson
An irritating kid in
Courtney's class

Mr. Garcia
Courtney's
third-grade
teacher

**Sandy Willen
and Jefferson Caine**
Morning anchors
on the local news

TABLE OF

contents

stereo **AG** 86

AG 86 🎵 ♡ Courtney's Mix 😊 ⚡ stereo

Game Over

 *ockwockwockwockwockwockwockwock.* Nonstop electronic sounds pelted Courtney Moore's ears as she leaned into the PAC-MAN arcade game she was playing.

Wockwockwockwock.

PAC-MAN munched through a string of tiny dots on-screen, heading for two bright red cherries in the middle of the glowing maze.

Courtney tucked a loose curl back into her scrunchie without letting up on the joystick. She'd been playing for nearly an hour. Her feet were sore and her eyes were starting to swim, but she couldn't take a break now, no way. If she cleared this round, she'd get to Level Nine in PAC-MAN for the first time *ever.*

"Watch out!" yelled Courtney's friend Kip Tomatsu beside her, pointing at Inky, the greenish-blue ghost that was heading right for PAC-MAN. Courtney slammed the joystick right and up, dodging Inky as she zipped through the game's maze, on the run.

Kip pushed his floppy hair out of his face, his eyes

glued to PAC-MAN's every move. "There's a power pellet on your right!" he shouted.

Courtney throttled right, seeing it—but as she did, Blinky, the red ghost, came out of nowhere.

Don't panic, she told herself, swerving left to avoid Blinky. *This always happens on Level Eight.*

"This always happens on Level Eight," Kip said.

"I know," Courtney replied, eyeing a large dot a few turns away on the maze. "I just need to get to that power pellet."

Kip nodded. He understood her strategy: Once she ate the power pellet, the ghosts would all turn dark blue, and then PAC-MAN could eat *them*, gobbling up points.

"You're almost done!" Kip whispered excitedly.

Courtney smiled, her eyes fixed on the screen. PAC-MAN was Courtney's favorite game, and Smiley's Arcade in the Orange Valley Mall was her favorite place to play. The games were brighter and louder here than on her TV at home, and being in a crowd of kids all trying to beat their high score felt exhilarating, like swimming in a crashing sea of flashing light and electronic sound effects.

"You're gonna get eaten!" Kip yelled, jolting Courtney out of her mini-trance. A trio of ghosts were almost on top of PAC-MAN.

Courtney yanked the joystick left, and PAC-MAN

munched down on the flashing power pellet. In a flash the ghosts turned dark blue, and Courtney changed direction so that PAC-MAN could crunch them up. As the ghosts disappeared, their point values flew up the screen, where they added to the game total.

"My highest score EVER!" Courtney whooped as the screen lit up with an electronic cascade of colors. Courtney high-fived Kip, pride surging through her. Neither of them had ever reached Level Nine before.

"Courtney!" someone called sharply.

Courtney knew who it was without looking. Sure enough, when she swiveled around, there was her step-sister, Tina, arms crossed and side ponytail bobbing impatiently.

"Time to go," Tina said, pointing at the giant digital clock by the arcade entrance.

"Five more minutes," Courtney pleaded. "I just beat my high score!"

"So?" Tina said, looking baffled.

Before Courtney could reply, PAC-MAN flashed, signaling the start of a new level.

Courtney whirled back to the screen. "Can't talk! Must play!" she yelped, rattling the joystick in a breakneck series of moves.

Tina put her hand on her hip. "We need to go, like,

now," she said. "We're meeting my dad at five thirty."

"One *second,*" Courtney replied, switching PAC-MAN's direction. But before she could make her next move, Tina leaned in front of the game screen.

"What are you DOING?!" Courtney shouted.

Tina's dark eyes scrutinized Courtney's hair. "Is that my scrunchie?" She said accusingly, eyeing the bright pink band on top of Courtney's head.

"I couldn't find any of mine this morning," Courtney explained, dodging both Tina and two ghosts converging on PAC-MAN. "This one was in the bathroom."

Courtney kept her eyes glued to the screen. Tina was the Queen of Scrunchies. She had at least twenty organized neatly in rainbow order on her side of the dresser, and there were always a few more on the counter in their shared bathroom. Was it so wrong for Courtney to borrow one when Tina had so many?

"I just got that scrunchie for Christmas! Give it back!" Tina said, blocking the entire screen.

"Get out of the way!" Courtney shouted, but it was too late.

WoowoowoowoowooWOCKWOCK, the game wheezed, letting out the sad electronic music that sounded when PAC-MAN died.

PAC-MAN's yellow circle body split open like a banana

〜〜 4 〜〜

peel and disappeared after Blinky gobbled him up. Courtney yowled in frustration as the words "GAME OVER" flashed on the screen.

"Uh-oh," Tina said, not sounding sad at all. "I guess now we can go."

◎

"Hurry up," Tina called over her shoulder as she sashayed past stores along the mall's second level.

Courtney hustled up next to her. "I am hurrying," she said, looking at her watch. "It's only five twenty-two anyway. I definitely had time to beat that last level."

Courtney turned to look at Tina, but Tina wasn't beside her. Instead, her stepsister had stopped to window-shop at the Gap. As usual when Tina became interested in something, she conveniently forgot they were on a schedule.

Courtney swallowed her frustration. Officially, she and Tina were at the mall "together." What that really meant was that Courtney hung out at the arcade while Tina prowled the mall and drank soda at the food court with her friends.

It hadn't always been this way. When they first met, Courtney was five and Tina was nine and they liked doing stuff together. They rode bikes, traded stickers, and swam in the pool in Tina's backyard. Tina even played My Little Pony with Courtney. When Courtney's mom and

Tina's dad, Mike, got married, Courtney felt like she had a sister.

Things started to change when their little brother, Rafi, was born. Courtney moved into the room Tina had had since she was a baby, and Tina did not like sharing it. She complained that Courtney was messy, and she got irritated if Courtney left even one sock on Tina's side of the room. But sometimes, when one of her favorite songs came on the radio, Tina would start dancing and insist that Courtney join in. Courtney felt like there were two Tina's: an angry Tina and a fun Tina. Courtney never quite knew which one she was going to get.

"Come on!" Courtney called. But now Tina was talking to someone and ignoring Courtney. So Courtney headed for the escalator without her.

Courtney's stepdad's store, D'Amico's Electronics, was on the third level. When she reached the store, Courtney saw a large "After Christmas Sale" sign hanging in the front window. Mike was behind the counter chatting with a lanky young man in a store T-shirt when Courtney entered. A moment later, Tina came in with the girl she had been talking to outside the Gap.

"Kiddos!" Mike greeted them. "This is Ben, the new assistant manager," he said, gesturing at the young man. "Ben, these are my daughters, Tina and Courtney."

"Wait—this is your *sister*?" Tina's friend said as Mike went to help a customer. "I wouldn't have guessed—you look so different."

"We're not *real* sisters," Tina said. "Courtney's my *step*sister."

Courtney blinked in surprise, her cheeks stinging with embarrassment. She looked away so that Tina wouldn't see how much the comment had hurt her feelings.

Mike came back to the counter. "Okay, kiddos," he said cheerfully. "Since you're still on Christmas break, I thought we could have movie night tonight. Check out what I picked up at the video store at lunch." He pulled two VHS tapes from behind the counter.

Courtney brightened. *The Goonies* was her favorite movie.

"Nerd flick," Tina muttered. Her friend laughed.

"I heard that," Mike said. "And I am not a nerd." He winked at Courtney. "For those of you with different tastes, how about..." he slowly revealed the second tape.

Tina smiled. "*Footloose*! Thanks, Dad."

A New Job

As they walked to the parking lot, Courtney told Mike that she'd reached Level Nine in PAC-MAN.

"No way," Mike said. "Level Nine? That's awesome."

Courtney nodded. "If I play every weekend, I bet I can finish *all* the levels by the end of the year—maybe even by the end of the summer!" Courtney said hopefully, watching her stepdad unlock his brown Chevy truck.

"Sounds like a good goal," Mike said.

Once they'd piled in, Mike navigated the truck into the after-work traffic. A few miles later, he turned off the busy road and drove through a residential area where soaring palm trees lined the streets. Courtney had lived in Orange Valley all her life. She had moved only once, after Mom and Mike got married, into Mike and Tina's house. It had been hard for Courtney to leave her old neighborhood and friends. Luckily, she'd met Sarah Barrett the day after she'd moved, and the two had been best friends ever since.

When Mike pulled into the garage, Courtney saw that her mom's car was still gone. That meant she was still working. Mom was the assistant director of Orange Valley parks and recreation, so she often had community meetings in the evenings.

Inside, Courtney kicked off her shoes. "What's for dinner?" she asked Mike.

"Your mother's tuna noodle casserole!" Mike said as he headed for the kitchen.

Courtney went into the family room, where Tina already had the TV tuned to MTV. A skinny guy was walking across a swimming pool, singing a song called "Magic." He was part of a group called The Cars. When that video ended, a new one started. This one had a band wearing red LEGO-looking blocks on their heads. Courtney was thinking how strange it was when the front door opened and a small voice called out, "Cor-ney?"

"Rafi!" Courtney called back. She hurried into the hall, where her little brother threw himself into her arms.

"Hey honey," Mom greeted Courtney wearily, as she set down her briefcase and slipped off her heels. Mom took Rafi to day care on her way to work every day and then picked him up on her way home.

Mike popped his head out from the kitchen. "Hey, buddy," Mike said to Rafi. Then he flashed a grin at Mom. "Welcome home! The dinner you made is almost ready."

"How was work?" Mom asked Mike later, as they sat around the table eating steamed carrots and casserole.

"Totally gnarly," Mike replied. Tina rolled her eyes at his attempt to sound like a teenager. "How was your day?" Mike asked, cocking an eyebrow at Mom. "Did you do it?"

"I did," Mom said.

"Do what?" Courtney asked, perking up. It bugged her when adults talked in code as if they thought kids wouldn't notice.

"*Tell* us!" Tina huffed. Rafi stuck out his lower lip, imitating her, which made Mom laugh.

"Do you remember last month, when Mayor Alvarez announced that he was resigning due to health issues?" Mom asked.

Courtney nodded and Tina shook her head at the exact same moment.

"The city's going to have a special election to replace him." Mike continued. "Guess who's going to run?"

"Who?" Courtney said, puzzled. Did they really think she would know who was running for mayor?

"Me!" Mom said, breaking into a smile.

"Really?" Tina said. She looked like Mom had just announced she was going to visit the moon.

Mom nodded. "I filed the papers today, and my name

will officially be added to the list of candidates tomorrow."

"That's great!" Courtney exclaimed.

"Thanks, Courtney," said Mom. "Jackie Barrett's going to be my campaign manager."

Jackie Barrett was Sarah's mom. She owned a bakery and was full of boundless energy. She was always volunteering for causes she believed in.

"I don't understand," Tina said, looking from Mom to Mike. "Why would you want to run for mayor?"

"Duh. Mike just said Orange Valley needs a new mayor," Courtney pointed out.

"No duh," Tina said. "That's not what I meant."

"I think Tina's wondering why I would want to be mayor," Mom explained. Tina nodded.

"Running for public office is something I've been considering for years, actually," Mom said, spooning more noodles onto Rafi's plate. "I've just never had the right opportunity."

"Until now," Mike agreed. "Maureen's got the right experience to lead Orange Valley toward the future."

Tina crossed her arms, still looking skeptical. "You already have a job," she told Mom. "Why would you want another one?"

"Because it's another chance to make a difference," Mom answered earnestly.

Mike nodded. "Maureen could be Orange Valley's first female mayor," he said proudly. "Just like Sandra Day O'Connor was the first female Supreme Court justice, or Geraldine Ferraro was the first woman nominated for vice president."

"The point is that I want to have a voice in shaping the issues I care about," Mom said.

"Like the environment?" Courtney asked. Mom made them save every newspaper and rinse every can and bottle. Every few weeks she and Courtney took them to the recycling center so that they wouldn't end up in a landfill.

"Exactly," Mom said. "I think the city could start a curbside recycling program."

"Maybe you could figure out what to do about the hole in the ozone layer," Courtney suggested. "We learned about it last year at school, and it's a huge problem."

Tina scoffed. "The hole in the ozone is, like, an *Earth-wide* problem. Maureen couldn't fix that, even if she was mayor."

"It's true that I couldn't fix the *whole* ozone problem by myself," Mom admitted, "but as mayor, I could make sure that the city's not doing things to make the hole *worse*."

"How would you do that?" Courtney asked.

"We could ban aerosol can sales within the city limits, for one," Mom said.

Tina gasped. "Like Aqua Net?" she asked. "So if you

become mayor, I'm going to have to, like, take the bus to Los Angeles to buy hair spray?" Courtney had seen Tina use half a can of Aqua Net on just one hairdo.

Mom laughed. "I'll have to win the election first."

Courtney put her fork down. "How many other people are running?" she asked.

"Four so far," Mom replied.

Courtney was surprised. Her mother would have to beat four other people? Could she do it? Suddenly, Courtney hated the thought of her mother losing. She imagined Mom as a fighter in the arcade game Karate Champ, doing flying circle kicks and vanquishing the other wannabe mayors. But what if . . .

"What if you don't get enough points?" Courtney blurted out. Mom, Mike, and Tina looked at her strangely.

"I mean *votes*," Courtney said quickly, her cheeks growing hot. "What if you don't get enough votes?"

"Then I'll lose," Mom replied. "I can't focus on that, though. I need to put my energy into campaigning." Mom paused. "And that means I need everyone's help."

"Sure," Courtney agreed.

Tina narrowed her eyes. "Help with what?" she asked.

"Chores around the house," Mike explained. "Laundry. Cleaning. Cooking. Maureen usually takes care of most of it, but we *all* need to pitch in and work as a team."

Tina opened her mouth to say something, but Rafi started banging his sippy cup on his high chair tray. "Team!" he shouted.

Courtney smiled. "We're on your team, Mom!" she agreed.

Dream Big
⚡ CHAPTER 3 ⚡

Four days later, when Courtney arrived at school, her classroom looked entirely different. The projects that had decorated the bulletin boards before the holiday break were gone. In their place, Courtney's teacher, Mr. Garcia, had put up posters of outer space. A series of photos now hung on the wall behind Mr. Garcia's desk: five men and two women, all smiling, wearing identical blue jumpsuits and holding space helmets.

"Welcome back!" Mr. Garcia greeted students as they took their seats. Mr. Garcia was everyone's favorite third-grade teacher because he made school fun. He had shaggy dark hair and a mustache and beard, and he liked to wear Hawaiian shirts or suspenders—sometimes both at the same time. Today he was wearing a red shirt with yellow pineapples and rainbow suspenders with a "Save the Whales" button.

As the students got settled, Mr. Garcia closed the classroom door. "I hope everyone had a fun break," he said. Then he did an effortless moonwalk back to his desk.

"What, you think I'm too old to break-dance?" Mr.

Garcia said when the kids laughed. "I'm trying to get you all psyched for the big event of 1986!"

"What big event?" Sarah asked.

"The *Challenger* launch!" Mr. Garcia said.

"The space shuttle?" another kid asked.

"Yes! The twenty-fifth space shuttle mission," Mr. Garcia explained. "The *Challenger* is launching on January twenty-third. That means *we* need to get prepared."

"For what?" Courtney asked. "We're not getting shot up into outer space."

"Maybe not," Mr. Garcia acknowledged, "But Christa McAuliffe *is*." He pointed to a photo on the wall of a woman with curly brown hair. "She's a high school teacher. When she goes into orbit, she'll become the first teacher *ever* to go into space!" Surprised murmurs rippled through the room. "To honor that achievement," Mr. Garcia went on, "thousands of kids in schools across the country are going to watch the shuttle launch live on television—including our school!"

Courtney glanced at Kip. They were huge Star Wars fans and had seen the movies together dozens of times.

Kip raised his hand and said, "If a teacher's going to

space, they should send some students, too. I'll go!"

The class laughed. "Well, no students this time, Kip," Mr. Garcia explained. "But Mrs. McAuliffe will be doing experiments in space, and they'll be taped so that we can watch them." He paused and waggled his eyebrows. "And, on day four, Mrs. McAuliffe will teach from space! We'll watch that live, just like the launch."

"Whoa. That's so cool." Sarah grinned.

"I know!" Mr. Garcia replied, snapping his suspenders. "Now, Christa McAuliffe won't be the first American woman to go into space—that was Sally Ride—but Mrs. McAuliffe will be the first civilian to make it out of the atmosphere." Mr. Garcia paused. "Women are achieving new milestones every day."

"Like your mom!" Sarah said to Courtney. Then she turned to Mr. Garcia. "Courtney's mom is running for mayor."

Mr. Garcia and the whole class turned to look at Courtney, who felt her face turn pink from the attention.

"She is?" Mr. Garcia asked. When Courtney nodded, Mr. Garcia beamed. "That's fantastic!" He snapped his suspenders again. "If she wins, I believe she'd become Orange Valley's first female mayor. That would be a historic accomplishment!"

Courtney looked at Christa McAuliffe's photo. Christa

reminded her of Mom. They both had curly hair and wide smiles, and they were both trying to accomplish big things.

"Your mom doesn't know how to be mayor," a kid named Justin Wilson told Courtney abruptly. He smirked, flipping up his shirt collar. "She works at a park."

Courtney was speechless, but Sarah whirled around in her chair to face Justin.

"Courtney's mom runs the whole parks *department*," Sarah snapped, "Besides, you probably don't even know what the mayor does."

"Yeah," Courtney echoed, grateful for her friend. Sarah never had a problem knowing what to say.

"My mom's worked on tons of political campaigns," Sarah continued, "and she thinks Courtney's mom could be the best mayor Orange Valley has ever had!"

"Whatever," Justin said. "It's not like—"

"Boys and girls," Mr. Garcia interrupted, "local politics are important, but let's get back to our space project. Take out your notebooks, please. I've got an assignment for you."

Justin Wilson is such a pain, Courtney thought as she opened a purple notebook to a clean page and wrote the date on the top line: January 6, 1986.

"The *Challenger* launch is an opportunity for us to think about what exploration and discovery mean in our own lives," Mr. Garcia said enthusiastically. "You might not want to travel into space, but I bet that, like the astronauts, each of you has a dream of your own that you want to achieve." Mr. Garcia paused, and everyone looked at him, waiting. "So I want each of you to dream big and prepare a five-minute class presentation explaining your personal passion. You can use any medium you want—words, pictures, even music—but whatever you do, it has to be uniquely *you*."

Kip whipped around in his seat to face Courtney. "I'm gonna make a *movie*!" he whispered.

"Cool!" Courtney replied. As Kip turned back to the front, however, uncertainty formed a knot in her stomach. *What's my big dream?* she wondered. *Do I even have one?*

◎

"My movie's going to be a cross between *Ghostbusters* and *The Goonies*," Kip mused, poking a straw into his juice pouch during lunch in the cafeteria. "I bet my dad will let me use his Betamax video camera if I promise to be careful. I could even get Toby to be in it, too!"

"Toby—your *dog*?" Courtney asked, wrinkling her nose in surprise.

Across the table, Sarah said, "Since my big dream is to travel, I'm going to plan a trip around the world and include every place I want to visit."

"That sounds rad," Kip said.

"I know, right?" Sarah replied eagerly. "What are you going to do, Courtney?"

"I'm still thinking about it," Courtney said. She bit into her bologna and cheese sandwich, wondering if she was the only one in class who hadn't come up with an idea yet.

"Make sure you pick something you love," Sarah suggested. Sarah really enjoyed giving advice.

"But I love too many things," Courtney replied. "Movies, and music, and video games—" She gasped mid-sentence, hit by a blast of inspiration. "I know—I'll create my own video game!"

"That sounds super difficult," Sarah said.

"Yeah," Kip agreed. "I mean, you're a total PAC-MAN master, but do you know how to program a computer game?"

"I'm not going to actually *make* a computer game," Courtney clarified. "I'm going to think up the characters and the world and the rules, and then explain the game in my presentation."

"Ohhhh," Kip said. "That makes sense."

"Make sure you think up great bad guys," Sarah said importantly. "Something scary, like spiders."

"Or irritating," Courtney replied. "Like Justin Wilson." Courtney pictured a villain with a shirt collar standing up so tall that it blocked his face.

On the bus ride home, Courtney thought about her video game. She fished a notebook and pencil out of her backpack and turned to a clean page. Mr. Garcia had said the Dream Big project needed to be unique. *What does that mean for my game?* she wondered.

For one thing, Courtney thought as she began to draw, *the hero should be a girl.* She always ended up playing boy characters in games because there weren't any girls. Unless you counted Ms. PAC-MAN, but she was just a yellow circle with a bow on top.

Courtney decided her hero would be brave and adventurous. But what should she do? *Maybe she could be exploring outer space,* Courtney thought, remembering Christa McAuliffe. Suddenly, Courtney knew her hero's name. Crystal, in honor of Christa McAuliffe. Crystal Starshooter. That sounded like someone who belonged in a Star Wars movie. *Crystal could be discovering planets no one else has even heard of.*

Courtney stopped drawing and closed her eyes. Suddenly she was no longer on a bus—she was her game's hero, on a spaceship wearing a white space suit. Her name was boldly stitched on a patch on the front of her suit, and her space helmet had a heart with a lightning bolt through it to show she was brave *and* kind. Crystal Starshooter wore a grappling hook on her belt that she used to swing over acid rivers and across rock canyons. She carried a ray blaster, which she used to repel her foes. Crystal traveled the galaxy to discover and collect rare items that would save planet Earth.

Save it from what? Courtney wondered, frowning. Then she was hit with inspiration. *Solar radiation!*

Now she was Crystal Starshooter landing on the planet Blastus, searching for the mineral that would repair the hole in the Earth's ozone layer to protect it from the sun's dangerous rays. Just as she discovered the glowing copper rock, a team of aliens with tall shirt collars attacked. They were trying to keep the rock for themselves, but they were no match for Crystal Starshooter. She made it off Blastus with the mineral she needed, leaving plenty behind for the aliens. Now she steered her rocket back to Earth, racing to reach her beloved home in time to save it from being burned up by the sun.

Ideas fizzed and crackled in Courtney's mind like a lit sparkler. She was so busy imagining her game that she nearly missed her stop.

Making Room

That Saturday when Courtney woke up, something felt wrong. She lay on the top bunk, staring at the patterned wallpaper, listening to Tina singing along to the radio in the bathroom next door. *It's Saturday*, Courtney realized. *I should be at Dad's.*

For as long as she could remember, Courtney had spent every weekend with her dad. They played video games and went bowling. Sarah came for sleepovers, and Dad let them stay up late eating chips and making cootie catchers. Dad helped her with her homework, and every single Saturday morning, he made waffles.

Not anymore, Courtney thought sadly. *Today's the day Dad moves.*

The whir of a car engine sounded in the street below. Courtney climbed down from her bunk and looked out the window. Her dad had just pulled up in his red Camaro. A month ago, Dad had gotten a new job as a software engineer at a computer company in Bellington, more than three hundred miles away from Orange Valley. It was a big promotion, so Dad had to move.

The car door opened and Dad's long legs poked out. He wore a shiny blue track suit and old running shoes. He reached into the Camaro's backseat and pulled out a metal animal cage.

Parsley! Courtney thought, her spirits lifting. Parsley was her guinea pig. He'd lived at Dad's ever since Dad had given him to her for Christmas a year ago. Now Parsley was coming to live at Mom's house.

Courtney threw on jeans and a T-shirt and dashed downstairs. Mom was holding the front door open for Dad and Parsley.

"Hey, Court!" Dad said, setting the cage down on the floor in the front hall. "Someone's excited to see you."

"Parsley," Courtney breathed, darting over to the cage. The plump caramel and white guinea pig looked up at her with dark chocolate eyes.

"I'm gonna miss this little dude," Dad chuckled, as Courtney opened Parsley's cage and scooped him up.

"He's going to miss you, too," Courtney replied. "We both are." She leaned against Dad, feeling like she was going to cry.

Dad put his arm around her. "We'll still see each other a lot."

"Not every weekend, though," Courtney said.

"True," Dad admitted, "but look at it this way. When

we do hang out, it'll be even *more* special and awesome."

Courtney nodded, wanting to believe this.

"Okay!" Dad said after a moment. "I have a couple of boxes of your stuff from my place in the trailer."

"We'll help you bring them in," Mom offered.

Courtney put Parsley back in his cage, and the three of them went out to the car. They carried the boxes upstairs to the room Courtney shared with Tina.

Tina was in her bathrobe with a thick towel wrapped around her head. "What is all that stuff?" she asked, clearly annoyed.

"Things from my room at my dad's," Courtney replied. "Clothes, books . . ."

Tina's nose crinkled in irritation. "Just make sure you keep it all on your side," she said, turning her back on Courtney.

Courtney knew Tina was upset that she no longer had a room to herself on the weekend. *How does she think **I** feel?* Courtney thought, frustration burning inside her. *I don't have my own room anymore either.*

Dad carried in one last box. "I should hit the road," he said.

"Okay," Courtney said reluctantly. She followed him out to his car.

"I'll call you when I get there," Dad told Courtney at

the curb. He gave her a hug
and a kiss on the forehead;
then he got in his car and
rolled down the window.

"What are you going
to listen to?" Courtney asked. Dad's
joke was that it was physically impossible
for him to drive unless there was music playing.

"Huey Lewis and the News," Dad said. He turned
the key and the sound of his favorite band kicked in on
the car stereo. "I made you a copy," Dad said, handing
Courtney a tape.

Courtney couldn't help but smile. "Thanks, Dad."

"I'll see you in a few weeks!" Dad yelled over the
power chords. "Call me anytime you want to talk."
Courtney nodded. She waved at her dad as he drove off
and the Camaro turned the corner out of sight.

Mom was waiting in the front hall when Courtney
came inside. "How are you?" she asked.

Courtney shrugged. Her parents had been divorced
since she was two, and she couldn't remember a time
when she hadn't spent the weekend with her dad. "I just
wish I could see him more than once a month," Courtney
whispered.

Mom wrapped her in a hug. "Believe me, your father

wishes that too," Mom said. "Sometimes people have to make choices that are better for their family in the long run but that make things more difficult in the moment. Moving to Bellington was that kind of a choice for your dad."

"At least I'll get to see Parsley every day now," Courtney said. "Can you help me carry his cage up to my room?"

Upstairs, Courtney could hear Tina singing along to Madonna's "Borderline." Mom swung open the bedroom door, and Tina stopped abruptly as Mom and Courtney stepped into the room carrying the cage.

"Um, I'm not sure what you guys are thinking, but there's no way I'm sharing my room with that . . . *rodent*," Tina announced.

"His cage was always in my room at Dad's house," Courtney protested, looking at Mom to back her up.

"He'll make a mess," Tina pointed out.

"I'll clean it up," Courtney promised.

"He *smells*," Tina said.

"I'll keep him on my side of the room," said Courtney.

"*Smells* don't stay on one side of a room," Tina scoffed. She gave a melodramatic sniff. "Also, I think I'm allergic."

"You are *not*," Courtney insisted. "And Parsley's part of the family."

"So am I!" Tina shot back.

"Time-out, you two," Mom said. "Tina, I understand

that you're not a big fan of Parsley, but he is Courtney's pet. Why don't we start with Parsley in your room and see how it goes?"

Tina scowled.

"In exchange, Courtney," Mom added, "you'll need to clean Parsley's cage three times a week to make sure it doesn't smell."

"Ugh, really?" Courtney asked. She only cleaned the cage once a week at Dad's house.

Mom nodded. "Does that work for you, Tina?"

"I guess," Tina grumbled, "but it still feels unfair."

"Well, it's a compromise," Mom said. "Let's try it for a week. If you find that having Parsley as a roommate is unbearable, we'll discuss it again. Right now, though, Courtney's missing her dad, and having Parsley close by will make her feel better."

"What's going to help *me* feel better?!" Tina retorted. Before anyone could respond, she stomped out of the room.

A while later, Courtney went downstairs and saw Tina sitting in the backyard by the pool. Mike was talking with her. Courtney couldn't hear what they were saying, but it didn't look like Tina was feeling much better.

◎

Courtney spent most of the day in her room with Parsley. Tina went to her friend Vanessa's house, but Rafi was excited about the new pet. Courtney taught him how to hold Parsley, and she let Rafi feed Parsley bits of carrot. Parsley had a mohawk-like cowlick that shook when he ate, which Rafi thought was hilarious. Rafi's giggles made Courtney laugh. Playing with him helped take Courtney mind off the fact that her dad was gone and her sister didn't like her.

After dinner, Courtney got into her pajamas, sat in her beanbag chair with Parsley on her lap, and listened to the Huey Lewis and the News tape her dad had given her. After the third song, Courtney heard Tina come up the stairs and go into the bathroom. A few minutes later, Tina came into their bedroom wearing her pajamas. She took one look at Parsley's cage and stomped over to Courtney.

"Why is that cage right next to the bed?" Tina demanded.

Courtney shrugged. "That's the only place it would fit."

"Well, it has to fit someplace else," Tina announced. "I am *not* sleeping with that thing right by my head." Tina turned and flounced out of the room, calling for her dad.

Courtney sighed and hugged Parsley, who gave her finger a gentle nuzzle. "You're so cute and sweet," Courtney told him. "Tina just needs to get to know you. Once she does, she'll love you as much as Rafi and I do."

Courtney put Parsley back in his cage. *If I move my desk closer to the dresser,* she thought, *I could squeeze Parsley's cage*

*"I am **not** sleeping with that thing right by my head,"* Tina announced.

over there. As Courtney started shoving the desk over, Mike poked his head into the room.

"Moving Parsley's house?" he asked. "Can I help?"

Courtney nodded. As Mike picked up the cage, Courtney said, "Why does Tina hate pets?"

"I don't think she hates them," Mike answered, putting Parsley's cage in its new spot. "She's just never had one. Her mom had a lot of allergies, so we never had animals in the house."

"I didn't know that," Courtney said softly. Tina's mom had died when Tina was six. Tina didn't talk about her very much. "I don't want Tina to be mad at me. I just want her to give Parsley a chance."

Mike nodded. "She will. It takes Tina some time to get used to new situations." Mike paused. "You know, you and Tina have both faced big changes in your families. You're alike in many ways."

Courtney was surprised. "We are?"

"You both miss someone you love," he said. He looked over to where Tina kept a photo of her mom taped to the wall. "And you're both doing the best you can to adjust. Try to be patient with each other."

Courtney nodded. She hoped Tina could be patient, too.

Totally Bogus
⚡ CHAPTER 5 ⚡

The next morning, Courtney took Parsley out of his cage and took him down to the family room. She and Rafi were going to set up an obstacle course of toilet paper tubes and crinkled paper for Parsley to run through. She hoped Tina would enjoy watching, too.

The phone rang as Courtney was gathering supplies. It was Kip, calling with big news.

"I just got Super Mario Brothers!" he crowed. "Wanna come over and play?"

"Yes!" Courtney said, excitement zinging down her spine.

"Great, I'm home until noon," Kip told her.

I'll make the obstacle course later, Courtney thought as she hung up the phone. Just then the doorbell rang. Courtney opened the door, still holding Parsley, and there was Jackie Barrett carrying a coffee cake and a giant binder.

"Hey Courtney!" Jackie chirped. "I'm here to talk campaign details with your mom."

"Come on in," Courtney said, stepping aside for Mrs. Barrett.

Mom came down the stairs. Courtney was surprised to see her dressed in a dark skirt and a blouse with a big bow at the neck. Her wavy, shoulder-length hair was puffed up high on her head like a helmet.

"I have the design for the campaign buttons," Jackie announced. She handed Mom a piece of paper. "What do you think?"

"*Maureen for mayor*," Mom read.

"That's cool," Courtney said enthusiastically.

"Makes my campaign sound official," Mom agreed.

"Mom, can I go over to Kip's to play Super Mario Brothers?" Courtney asked.

Mom looked surprised. "Not now, honey. The photographer's coming to take campaign photos this morning, remember? The whole family has to be here."

"Oh, right," Courtney said. "So that's why you look like you're dressed for work on a Sunday."

"You should get dressed, too," Mom said, checking her watch. "I got you a new dress. It's in your room. Make sure you put Parsley back in his cage."

In her bedroom, Courtney found Tina standing in front of the mirror, her long hair twisted up in Hot Sticks rollers. She was wearing a blue floral dress and a sour expression.

Tina glanced at Parsley and shuddered. "Put that thing away!" Then she nodded toward the closet, where an identical blue dress was on a hanger. "Your mom wants us to wear matching dresses for this picture," Tina said flatly as Courtney put Parsley in his cage.

Courtney loved the dress—especially the puffy short sleeves and the fancy lace collar. It was a Laura Ashley, and Courtney had always wanted one. She couldn't wait to try it on.

After she changed, Courtney headed back downstairs. As she was leaving, Tina was unwrapping the rollers from her hair. "Why do I even bother," Courtney heard Tina sigh. "There's barely any curl at all."

"Cor-ney!" Rafi cooed from his high chair as Courtney came into the kitchen. Mike was at the kitchen counter, wearing a suit Courtney didn't even know he owned.

"Snazzy dress!" Mike told Courtney as he spooned yogurt into a bowl.

"Snazzy suit," Courtney replied, doing a twirl. She sat down at the table and watched Mike feed Rafi for a while.

"When will the photographer be here?" Courtney asked. She wished she was at Kip's house playing Super Mario Brothers.

"Soon," Mike said. "Can you go see if Tina's ready?"

Courtney nodded. She hurried up the steps, hoping there might still be time to go to Kip's after the photos. When she got to her bedroom, it was empty, but she could hear Tina's voice coming from behind the closed bathroom door. "I *know*! It's totally bogus."

For a moment, Courtney was confused. Who was Tina talking to? Then she noticed that the cord from the telephone in their bedroom was stretched from the wall jack all the way under the bathroom door. Tina started talking again. Courtney crept forward, straining to hear.

"She's, like, a *total* dweeb," Tina was saying. "Dude, I'm not kidding! I could deal with sharing a room when she went to her dad's on the weekends. But now she's going to be here, like, *all the time*. And she's such a slob."

Courtney turned away from the bathroom door and glanced into their room. Tina's bed on the bottom bunk was neatly made. The books and papers on Tina's desk were in tidy stacks. Her jewelry and scrunchies were all sorted by color on her side of the dresser.

Courtney's upper bunk was a tangle of sheets and pillows. Her desk was scattered with notebooks, colored pencils, plastic baggies full of quarters, and her diary. Next to the desk, Parsley's cage balanced on a couple of milk crates. The floor around it was covered in shredded paper bedding, guinea pig pellets, and a chunk of gnawed cucumber.

So Tina's a neat freak, Courtney thought defiantly. *That doesn't make me a dweeb!*

"And the rodent? It *smells*!" Tina continued from the bathroom. "Courtney, like, takes it out of its cage and lets it run around. It totally gets into her stuff. If that thing poops on any of my stuff, it's dead!" She paused. "Totally. I think all Courtney cares about is that grody guinea pig and her pathetic arcade games."

Courtney froze. Parsley was not grody, and arcade games were not pathetic.

"Tina," Mike called from the kitchen. "Are you ready?"

The bathroom door swung open, and Courtney found herself nose to nose with her stepsister.

"What are you doing?" Tina spluttered. "Were you *eavesdropping* on me?!" Before Courtney could answer, Tina slammed the door.

Less Than Perfect

I t was windy outside, but Courtney barely noticed. She was sitting on a lawn chair as the wind blew her curls around her face. Tears stung her eyes, but she wiped them away, trying to forget what Tina had said about her.

What would Crystal Starshooter do if she was attacked unexpectedly? Courtney wondered, picturing her game hero. *Crystal wouldn't be afraid, and she wouldn't back down. She'd stand up to anyone.*

Courtney imagined Crystal Starshooter facing an evil alien princess who wore her long dark hair in a side ponytail and ruled a neon-bright planet called Malltron. The princess announced that all pets were to be banished from her kingdom. The villagers begged Crystal to save their beloved animals from the cruel princess.

Crystal Starshooter swooped into the Malltron palace as the evil princess was gliding down a glass staircase with colorful scrunchies lining the bannister. The princess sneered at Crystal and began throwing fiery Hot Sticks at her. But Crystal Starshooter dodged the princess's weapons and dove behind a potted plant. She pulled out her ray blaster and began firing with precision. *Bam! Bam! Bam!* One by one, Crystal blew the scrunchies off the banister. As each scrunchie exploded into a ball of fire, the evil princess screamed, "My scrunchies! Not my beautiful scrunchies!" While the princess wailed, Crystal raced to the dungeon and released the pets, sending them back into the arms of the happy villagers.

Suddenly the glass patio door slid open and Mike came outside.

"There you are!" Courtney's stepfather said, plopping down beside her. "The photographer is here. He's just setting up in the living room."

"Cool," Courtney whispered. She rubbed her eyes, trying to get rid of any evidence of crying.

Mike looked concerned. "You okay?" He asked. She nodded, but Mike raised a dubious eyebrow. "You don't look okay," he observed.

Courtney bit the inside of her lip. She wanted to tell Mike about the mean things Tina had said about her on the phone, but all the words she wanted to say were stuck together in a lump in her throat.

Before she or Mike could say anything else, the patio door opened again and Jackie Barrett poked her head out. "Ready to have your picture taken?"

When Courtney and Mike joined the rest of the family in the living room, Tina looked at Courtney like she had three heads. "What happened to your hair?" Tina asked.

Courtney checked her reflection in the mirror over the fireplace. Her hair had grown to twice its usual size from the wind! "Oh no—I look like a mad scientist!" Courtney wailed, tugging at her hair to tame it. She turned to Mike. "Why didn't you tell me?"

Mike looked confused. "I thought it was *supposed* to look like that."

"Don't panic," Mom said calmly. "We can fix this."

A few minutes later, Courtney was sitting on the couch while Mom spritzed her hair with water from a spray bottle and used a pick to tame her mountain of curls. Finally, she gathered it into a neat French braid.

"Better?" Mom asked, as Courtney checked the braid in the mirror.

"Better," Courtney said gratefully, giving her mom a big hug.

Across the room, Tina was sitting stiffly in a chair watching Courtney and Mom with an odd expression.

Courtney thought she almost looked sad. But when Tina noticed Courtney watching her, her expression changed to her familiar look of annoyance.

"Finally," Tina huffed. "Can we get this photo over with now?"

The photographer organized them in front of the fireplace. Mom stood in the middle, with Mike beside her holding Rafi, who was now sporting a tiny little bow tie. Tina and Courtney stood on opposite ends.

"Everyone smile! You're the perfect family!" The photographer crooned as he snapped away. But as she remembered Tina's sharp words, Courtney felt less than perfect.

By the time the photo shoot was over, it was too late for Courtney to go to Kip's house. Everyone changed their clothes, and Mom put Rafi down for a nap. Mike offered to drive Courtney and Tina to the mall.

As soon as they got there, Tina announced that she was meeting friends at Hot Dog on a Stick. She turned and left without another word.

"Be back here at four o'clock sharp," Mike called after her. He turned to Courtney and gave her a handful of quarters. "It's been a rough weekend, kiddo," he said. "Go play some games."

"Thanks, Mike," Courtney said. As she rode the

glass-walled escalator up to the arcade, Courtney pictured herself destroying the evil princess's scrunchies, but she didn't really feel any better. She knew she had to face the facts, and they weren't something that a video game could fix: Her sister—well, *step*sister—didn't like her anymore.

But why?

Challengers

On Monday morning, Tina's bed was already neatly made when Courtney woke up. There was a note taped to the bathroom mirror. *The cage STINKS*, it read. *CLEAN IT NOW!!!!!*

Courtney changed the bedding in Parsley's cage and gave him fresh water. Then she got dressed and went down to the kitchen for breakfast. Courtney got a bowl of cereal and sat down across from Tina, who was eating a Pop-Tart and reading a magazine. Neither of them spoke.

Mom came in and put Rafi in his high chair while Courtney poured Cheerios onto his tray. "O-O-Os," Rafi chanted.

"Thanks, sweetie," Mom said, pouring a cup of coffee. "Can you take care of the recycling out in the garage when you're done with breakfast? It's piling up out there."

"Sure, Mom," Courtney agreed.

"I know there's a lot," Mom added. "Tina, will you help too, please?" Mom asked.

Tina sighed, but after breakfast, she followed Courtney to the garage. "I don't know why we can't just put our trash out on the curb like everyone else does." Tina muttered. "This is such a waste of time."

Courtney didn't say anything as she lifted a bag of empty glass bottles out of a large garbage can. Then she put a new bag into the can.

Tina pulled a bag of aluminum cans out of another garbage can. "At least this stuff isn't smelly," she commented. Courtney stopped what she was doing and glared at Tina. Was she comparing Parsley to garbage?

Tina looked surprised. "What are you upset about?"

"Really?" Courtney asked in disbelief. "You called me a dweeb, and you insulted my pet. Don't you think that hurts my feelings?"

Tina paused. "I didn't know you were listening," she said. Then Tina rolled her eyes. "It's not like I *meant* it."

"Then why did you say it?"

Tina's face turned red. "You just don't understand."

Courtney frowned. "Understand what?"

"That it's hard for me to be in this family sometimes," Tina blurted out.

"What do you mean?" Courtney asked.

But Tina dropped her bag and launched herself back toward the house without another word.

◎

Courtney sat next to Kip on the bus to school. He spent

the whole ride giving her a play-by-play of how he'd beaten his high score in Super Mario Brothers the day before.

"It's different from playing Mario Brothers in the arcade," Kip said, hoisting his feet up on the hard pleather seat in front of them. "And I found some cool shortcuts."

Courtney nodded, half listening, as Kip talked about point totals and hidden level rewards. It was tough to focus, though. Her thoughts kept returning to what Tina had said that morning. What did Tina mean when she'd said it was hard for her to be in their family?

When they got to school, Mr. Garcia announced a new project. "Over the next few weeks, we're going to build a scale replica of the space shuttle. We should be finished by the time the shuttle takes off!" He distributed copies of the *Challenger* diagram and assigned each student a section to trace on cardboard, cut out, and paint.

"The shuttle is made up of thousands of parts," he said. "For *Challenger* to fly a successful mission, all the parts have to work together flawlessly, and so do the astronauts." Mr. Garcia pointed to the shuttle diagram. "Mrs. McAuliffe's lesson from space will include a tour of the shuttle. She'll explain what the crew's duties are and how they have to work as a team if they're going to achieve the goals of their mission."

Courtney thought about this as she started tracing her

payload door. She didn't have much experience being on a team. A lot of the stuff she liked to do, like playing video games, involved competing against people, not working with them. When Mom announced she was running for mayor, Mike had said their family needed to work as a team. After this morning's argument with Tina, though, Courtney didn't see how that could possibly happen.

When she got home that afternoon, Courtney flopped down on the sofa in the family room. She'd just pulled out her books to do homework when she heard another key turn in the front door. Tina came in a few moments later and immediately flipped on the TV.

"Um, I'm doing homework," Courtney pointed out.

"Video countdown's starting!" Tina said.

Courtney tried to focus on her fractions, but her concentration only lasted until a boppy electronic intro kicked in.

"It's Cyndi Lauper!" Tina said over the music. "Come on! You *have* to dance!" The angry Tina was gone. Courtney laughed as the fun Tina pulled her up, and the two started dancing.

Tina sang along to "Girls Just Wanna Have Fun." Courtney joined in. She knew she was off-key, but she didn't care. This was her favorite song.

Tina swung Courtney around until she was dizzy. They started giggling more than they were singing. Suddenly, Rafi appeared. "Cor-ney! Teeny!" he squealed. Rafi held his arms out and hopped from one foot to the other. "Rafi dance too!"

"We're home," Mom called over the music. She was carrying a bag of groceries, her briefcase, and Rafi's backpack.

Rafi kicked off his shoes and dance-galloped in a circle around his sisters. At the top of his two-year-old voice, he sang, "Girls have fun! Girls have fun!"

Courtney and Tina laughed. "That's right, Rafi," Tina said. "We just wanna have fun!"

Courtney sighed. Did this dance party mean that all was forgiven and Tina liked her again?

The next night, Mom had a campaign meeting after work, so Mike ordered pizza for dinner and they ate in front of the TV. As Mike took Rafi upstairs to bed, he said, "Don't forget your chores, girls."

Tina sighed dramatically. But since it was her turn to do laundry, she got to stay in front of the TV and fold clothes and towels.

It was Courtney's turn to clean up the kitchen. Mom didn't let them use paper plates, so there were still dishes

At the top of his two-year-old voice, Rafi sang, "Girls have fun!"

to wash, even when they ordered out.

When Courtney was done, she decided to call her dad. He'd only been gone for three days, but Courtney felt like she hadn't talked to him in weeks. His phone rang and rang, and finally, on the tenth ring, the answering machine picked up. After the beep, she said, "Hi, Dad. It's me. I . . . I just called to say hi. Um, I'll talk to you later. Okay. Bye."

Courtney hung up the phone and leaned her head against the receiver on the wall.

"Courtney?"

Courtney jumped at the sound of her name. She turned around. It was Mom. "I didn't hear you come in," Courtney said, giving her mom a hug. "I'm glad you're home."

"Me, too," Mom said brightly, going to the fridge. "Did you have dinner? Is Rafi in bed?" Mom grabbed a container of cottage cheese and a head of lettuce.

Courtney perched on a stool at the counter. "Yes and yes," she said as Tina came into the kitchen.

"Hi, Tina," Mom said, tearing lettuce leaves into a bowl. "I'm glad you're here. I have news." She sounded excited. *"Good Morning, Orange Valley!* asked me to come on for an interview as part of its series on the mayoral election."

Courtney gasped, "That's rad!" *Good Morning, Orange Valley!* was a local news show that aired live every weekday morning.

"*Very* rad," Mom said with a smile. "It'll be a great chance to talk about my ideas for the city. Do you girls want to go with me to the station?"

"Are you kidding? Yes!" Courtney squealed.

"What about you, Tina?" Mom asked.

Tina shook her head. "I don't think so." She turned and left the kitchen.

"I don't get it," Courtney said. "Tina is obsessed with television. Why would she turn down a chance to visit a real TV studio?"

Mom scooped cottage cheese onto the lettuce. "It's hard to say, but it's Tina's decision." Mom paused. "How are things going between you two?"

"It's hard to say," Courtney echoed. "Sometimes she's angry with me for no reason and sometimes she's nice to me. I never know which Tina it's going to be."

Mom sat down next to Courtney. "I'm sure that's confusing," she said. "Tina's mom's birthday is coming up. This is always a difficult time for Tina."

Courtney's breath caught in her throat. "Oh, gosh. I forgot." Courtney told her mom about what had happened in the garage that morning. "Tina said it's hard to be in this family sometimes."

"She did?" Mom looked sad as she put her hand on Courtney's. "Try to give Tina a little extra space right now."

Courtney nodded, wishing there was something else she could do for her stepsister.

The next afternoon, when Tina went to the mall with her friends, Courtney took the bus home. She wanted to do something to make Tina feel better. Mom had said to give her space. Courtney couldn't move out of their shared room, but she decided she could clean her side of it.

Courtney picked up the pile of books she'd left on the floor. She hung up all the clothes she'd flung over her desk chair. She made her bed, straightened her side of the dresser, and cleaned Parsley's cage, even though it wasn't that messy. Courtney even lugged the vacuum cleaner upstairs and sucked up all the crumbs from the carpet.

The last thing Courtney did was dust the shelves above the dresser. Tina had a collection of ceramic figurines that had belonged to her mom, and Courtney was careful as she swooshed the feather duster between them. As she finished the bottom shelf, the thud of a backpack hitting the floor made Courtney jump.

Courtney heard Tina shout, "What are you *doing*?" at the same moment she saw a purple penguin wobble. Courtney lunged frantically to catch the figurine, and she steadied it before it toppled.

That's when the handle of the feather duster caught the

edge of a carousel horse. The horse fell to the dresser and, with a *crack*, the tail broke off.

"Look what you *did*!" Tina screamed.

Courtney was horrified. "Tina, I'm so sorry. I didn't mean to—"

"—You broke it," Tina sobbed, picking up the brightly painted tail.

"I can fix it," Courtney stammered. She reached for the horse, but Tina yanked it away.

"No you can't! Get out!" Tina cried. "Just leave me alone."

Courtney was shaking as she backed out of the room. Tina slammed the door, and Courtney started crying. Trying to help had only created a bigger mess.

The Interview

Tina refused to speak to Courtney even after Mike helped Courtney glue the horse's tail back on. Courtney tried apologizing every day, but Tina just kept her headphones on and looked away. Tina spent the entire weekend at her friend Vanessa's house.

Monday was the day of Mom's interview, and Mom woke Courtney shortly after four a.m. They had to be at the studio by five o'clock. Courtney grabbed her blue Laura Ashley dress from the closet and changed in the bathroom.

When she got downstairs, Mom was drinking coffee and wearing an outfit Courtney had never seen before: a red skirt and matching jacket. The shoulder pads were so big they reminded Courtney of a football player.

"Is that new?" Courtney asked, taking the toast Mom handed her.

"It's a power suit," Mom said. "What do you think?"

"Does it give you power?" Courtney asked.

"I'm not sure," Mom admitted with a little laugh, "but I feel confident in it, and that's what counts."

It was still dark outside as they drove across town, and

there was hardly any traffic. At the studio, Mom buzzed a button at the door and a young woman wearing a headset and carrying a clipboard let them in. Courtney and her mom followed the woman down a long cement corridor into the studio. It was a big square room with a high ceiling hung with huge lights. There was a long, brightly lit desk in one corner, and next to it was a carpeted area with chairs and a low table. One wall was covered by a large green screen. There were enormous cameras on wheels, and thick cables crisscrossed the floor. More people in headsets bustled about.

A woman with long dark hair and a gray blazer was sitting at the desk, looking over some papers. "Hey, that's Sandy Willen—she's the morning anchor!" Courtney whispered to Mom.

"I know," Mom whispered back.

Suddenly, Sandy Willen was walking toward them. "Maureen?" she said, flashing a brilliant smile. "So lovely to meet you!" She shook Mom's hand.

"You, too," Mom answered. "This is my daughter, Courtney."

As Courtney shook Sandy's hand, she tried not to stare. Courtney had never met a news anchor before.

"I'm so glad you're here, Courtney! And I'm so glad you agreed to bring your *mom* with you," Sandy joked with a wink. "Jefferson!" She called to a man in a suit standing next to a television camera that was taller than Courtney.

"This is my coanchor, Jefferson Caine," Sandy said as he came over. "Jeff, this is candidate Maureen D'Amico and her daughter, Courtney."

"Pleased to meet you both," Jefferson Caine said, smiling. He was wearing makeup, and his teeth glowed an unnatural white.

"So we'll be reading the news for the first ten minutes, and after the first commercial break we'll do your inter-view," Sandy explained to Mom.

"Sounds good," Mom said. She fished out a short stack of index cards from her purse and started glancing through them.

"Try not to *read* anything as a response," Sandy advised Mom. "You'll be a lot more likable if you don't."

"Okay," Mom replied, but her eyes crinkled in worry.

Suddenly Sandy sucked in her breath. "My goodness, I just had a *brilliant* idea!" she announced to the room. "Maureen, Courtney should do the interview with you!"

Courtney caught her breath. Even in her wildest dreams, she'd never imagined she'd be *on* TV. She looked up at Mom. "Can I?" she whispered.

Sandy went on, not waiting for Mom's reply. "Maureen, this would give you a chance to show voters that you're not just a candidate—you're also a mom."

Mom nodded, but she looked concerned. She turned to Courtney and asked, "Sweetheart, are you sure you want to do this?"

"Totally," Courtney answered.

"Great!" Sandy said, clapping her hands together. "You two should get ready—makeup is that way."

Mom turned to Courtney as they headed to the makeup room. "If the reporters ask you a question, you'll need to answer," Mom told her. "Just speak up and say what you believe."

"I will," Courtney nodded, excitement shooting from her toes all the way up to the crown of her head. She was going to be on *television*!

In the makeup room, a woman put a little blush on Courtney, but Mom got a thick layer of foundation that hid her freckles.

A man wearing a headset walked them over to the carpeted area with the chairs. They watched the anchors take their seats behind the desk as two giant cameras got into position in front of them. Courtney could tell Mom was nervous because she kept wiping her hands on her skirt.

"Okay, folks," said the man with the headset, standing between the cameras. "We're live in five, four, three." Then he went silent and his fingers counted down two and one.

Courtney breathed as quietly as she could while Sandy and Jefferson delivered the morning news to the cameras. Ten minutes felt like ten seconds, and soon the anchors were hustling over to sit with Courtney and Mom, the lights bright on them all. Suddenly Courtney felt nervous. Maybe being on TV wasn't such a good idea.

"Welcome back, Orange Valley viewers!" Sandy said when they were live. "We're continuing our series of interviews with the candidates for Orange Valley mayor. Maureen D'Amico is the director of our town's Parks and Recreation Department and a mother of two!"

"Three actually," Mom corrected politely. "I also have a stepdaughter, Tina, who's thirteen."

"Okay," Sandy said. "Maureen, can you tell us a little about yourself? You've been divorced, I take it?"

Mom looked surprised at the question. "Yes, I have," she said. "I'm remarried with three children."

"Right, and your daughter Courtney is here as well. Courtney, what's it like being part of a blended family?" Sandy asked, suddenly turning to Courtney.

Courtney froze. She hadn't really expected Sandy to ask her a question. And why this question? What did their family have to do with the election?

Mom gave Courtney a smile. *Don't worry*, her eyes

seemed to say. *I'm right here.*

Courtney thought of how up-and-down the last few days with Tina had been, but she didn't think she should mention any of that on live television.

"Being in a blended family is fine," she said. "I mean, we're the same as any other family."

"I agree," Mom said. "Like every family, we have our challenges, but we learn from each other and support each other, and that helps strengthen our bonds."

Courtney swallowed and nodded. Inside, though, she couldn't help wondering: Was that really true? Were they really supporting and learning from each other?

Mom was talking about what her priorities would be as mayor, like starting a citywide recycling program and giving more money to the schools.

Jefferson Caine checked his notes. "One more question before we wrap up. How will you manage to be both a good mother *and* a good mayor?"

"Because that's a pretty tall order," Sandy added.

Frustration knotted up in Courtney's chest at Sandy Willen's words. Why didn't she think Mom could do a good job?

Mom answered the question calmly. "I know how to juggle responsibilities," she replied. "I'm organized and hardworking."

"Sure, sure," Sandy said, waving her hand like she was swatting away a fly. "But Orange Valley has never had a *mother* as mayor before. What if one of your children is sick when you have to attend an important meeting?"

"If one of us got sick, my mom would still be a good mayor," Courtney blurted out. "My stepdad Mike would take care of us. Mom works hard and always thinks about what's best for everyone. She cares about making Orange Valley a better place."

Courtney paused. The anchors looked surprised. So did Mom.

"Wow," Jefferson Caine said after a moment. "That's

quite an endorsement!" The adults all chuckled.

Courtney smiled, but a wisp of discomfort curled inside her. Had she just ruined Mom's chances to win the election?

◎

The sun was up and the street was full of traffic when Courtney and Mom walked out of the studio. Courtney had changed into school clothes in the studio bathroom, but mom was still wearing her power suit. "Did I say the wrong thing?" Courtney asked.

"Are you kidding? You were amazing, sweetheart," Mom said. "I don't think anyone was expecting you to chime in at that moment, but when you did, you spoke your mind—from your heart. That's what counts."

"I just want *everyone* to vote for you," Courtney said as they got in the car.

Mom put her hand on Courtney's. "We can't control how many people vote for me," Mom said calmly. "Some people may not. But I'm so pleased that you were confident enough to stand up for what you believe in. I'm proud of you."

"I'm proud of you, too," Courtney said.

◎

Mom dropped off Courtney at school on her way to work. The playground was filling up with students, and Sarah and Kip were playing hacky sack near the flagpole. They lit up when they saw Courtney coming.

"Great job on TV this morning," Sarah said. "What you said about your mom was awesome!"

"Really?" Courtney said, feeling relieved.

"Definitely," Kip echoed, pocketing the hacky sack. "You nailed it!"

"Thanks," Courtney said, but before she could say anything else, other kids rushed over.

"We saw you on *Good Morning, Orange Valley!*"

"You were tubular!"

"Is your mom really running for mayor?"

"I can't believe you were on TV. Were you nervous?"

Justin Wilson pushed through the crowd. "Hey, Moore!" he called to Courtney. "I saw you on TV. At least I thought it was you. The girl looked like you, but she talked a lot more than you ever do," Justin smirked.

Courtney's cheeks grew hot, but she couldn't think of a good comeback.

Sarah put a hand on her hip. "Courtney talks when she has something to say. Unlike some people who just like to hear the sound of their own voice."

Justin shrugged and crossed his arms over his chest. "My dad says all politicians are the

same. They tell lies to get elected, but then they don't do anything."

Courtney felt the same fire in her chest that she had at the TV studio. "My mom's not a politician," Courtney retorted, her eyes flashing. "She's running for mayor because she wants to *do* something—not just talk about what someone else should do."

Before Justin could respond, the bell rang. As kids scattered, Kip nodded at Justin. "You got burned, Wilson."

Sarah looped her arm through Courtney's as they followed Kip through the door. "See, Courtney?" Sarah said, beaming. "When you do speak up, you know exactly what to say."

Courtney smiled shyly. *If only I knew what to say to Tina*, she thought.

Angry Tina
and Fun Tina

That afternoon, Courtney was doing homework at the kitchen table when Tina blew through the front door. She came into the room and dropped her backpack on the chair across from Courtney.

Courtney expected Tina to ignore her. Instead, Tina reached into her backpack, pulled out a package of gummy bears, and stretched her arm out to Courtney. "Here."

It took Courtney a second to realize Tina was offering her the bag.

"Really?" Courtney said, surprised. Gummy bears were her all-time favorite candy. Tina loved them, too. She loved them so much that she never shared them with anyone.

"I got them for you," Tina said, tossing the bag on the table.

"Why?" Courtney asked, folding her arms skeptically.

Tina went quiet for a moment.

"I liked what you said on TV this morning," she said at last. "It was annoying when those reporters asked Maureen if she could be a good mom and a good mayor at the same time. She can be both, duh!"

"Totally," Courtney said.

Tina picked up her backpack. "You were right to defend your mom. So I got you some candy." Then she turned and headed for the front hall.

"Thanks," Courtney called after Tina.

"Don't eat 'em all at once or you'll get a massive sugar headache," Tina said, and then bolted up the stairs.

◎

Courtney hoped Tina's gummy-bear gift meant they were friends again, but Tina didn't say much to Courtney— or anyone—for the rest of the week.

On Friday, Courtney was sitting on the floor in the family room playing with Rafi while Tina watched MTV. Suddenly, Mike let out a whoop in the kitchen.

"Maureen just called from the office," he said, coming into the family room. "Her dinner meeting got canceled. She's on her way home!"

Rafi got so excited that he knocked down the block tower he'd been building with Courtney. "Mama!" he squealed.

"Great!" Courtney said, relieved. All week, Mom had had evening campaign events. Mike picked up Rafi from day care and fed him dinner in the kitchen, but he'd let Courtney and Tina eat in front of the TV. After the second night of Tina's silence, Courtney started eating in the kitchen with Rafi. Mike talked to Courtney about her day, and Rafi made her laugh, and it was much better than enduring angry Tina. But it still didn't feel the same without Mom.

"I have decided," Mike announced, "that I am going to cook a fancy family dinner in honor of Maureen being home."

"Um, are you sure you can handle that?" Courtney said.

"Yes," Mike replied, sounding mildly offended. "Let me remind you that I've made dinner every night this week."

"Yeah, right," Tina replied. "You made mac and cheese from a box and ordered pizza. I'm not sure that counts as cooking." For the first time in days, Tina looked at Courtney. The two of them exchanged a concerned glance.

"I made hot dogs, too," Mike said.

"Yeah, but that set off the smoke alarm," Courtney reminded him.

"For like two seconds!" Mike protested. "Listen, I can program a twenty-one-function remote control in less than a minute. I can definitely make dinner for my family."

"What are you going to make?" Tina asked.

"I'm glad you asked," Mike said enthusiastically. "The menu includes pork chops, baked potatoes, corn on the cob, dinner rolls, and fruit salad. I hope you're all hungry," he called, heading back into the kitchen.

As Rafi returned to his blocks, Tina said, "My dad's not great at cooking more than one thing at a time."

"Maybe we should help him," Courtney suggested.

"You'll probably just break something," Tina muttered. "That's what you did when you tried to help me."

Courtney sighed. "I *was* trying to help," she said. She was afraid her stepsister would storm off, but Tina stayed on the sofa, her eyes glued to the TV. "I said I was sorry, like, a million times," Courtney went on. "And Mike and I fixed the horse."

"You shouldn't have broken it in the first place," Tina replied.

"Well, I did." Courtney said, exasperated. "It wasn't on purpose, and I didn't do it to hurt you. I was trying to be nice by cleaning our room."

Tina shrugged. Courtney's next words came out in a flood before she could stop them. "I know you're having a rough time right now, but you know what, Tina? You make it really hard to be nice to you sometimes."

Tina looked surprised and a little sad, too. But before she could reply to Courtney, Rafi tugged on Courtney's arm. "Cor-ney! Blocks!"

Tina frowned and turned back to MTV while Courtney returned to playing with Rafi.

Half an hour later, there was a crash in the kitchen.

"Everything okay, Mike?" Courtney called.

"Fine!" Mike called back. Moments later, Courtney smelled something burning.

Courtney ran to the kitchen. When she opened the door, she started coughing. The kitchen was thick with smoke, and the room was a mess. The counters were covered with dirty cutting boards and plates. Raw pork chops sat on a broiler pan on the stove top, beside a large pot of water bubbling maniacally. Mike was kneeling on the floor wearing oven mitts and prying half-burned dinner rolls off a metal cookie tray.

"Hey guys!" Mike said, glancing up as Courtney came in. Tina was behind her, carrying Rafi. Mike was wearing mom's pink apron, and he had a sweat-soaked bandanna tied around his head like Ralph Macchio in *The Karate Kid*. He looked frazzled. "Everything's under control, don't worry!" he sputtered, struggling to his feet.

"Things don't look under control," Courtney noted.

"At all," Tina added.

"They are," Mike insisted. "We're just not having dinner rolls tonight."

Mike yanked off his bandanna and mopped his face with it. Courtney couldn't help but feel bad for him.

"Let us help, Dad," Tina said.

"Really?" Mike sounded relieved. "That would be awesome."

"I'll do the corn," Tina offered. She put Rafi down and moved to the counter without waiting for Mike to agree.

"And Rafi and I will set the table," Courtney added, taking her brother's hand.

Everyone had a job to do, and soon the kitchen hummed with activity. Mike seasoned the chops and cut fruit for the salad. Tina shucked the corn and put the ears into the pot of boiling water. Courtney put out plates, and Rafi followed her with cloth napkins. Tina came over and helped them count out silverware. Rafi held up a spoon like it was a microphone. He started singing and dancing, and Tina and Courtney started laughing. They hadn't laughed together in a long time, Courtney realized.

Just as Mike got the pork chops in the oven, Courtney heard the front door open. Mom was home!

"Hey guys," Mom said, padding wearily into the kitchen. She stopped short, noticing the disarray. "Goodness, what *happened*?"

"We made dinner! Together!" Courtney said, beaming. She rattled off the menu.

"Wow," said Mom, looking impressed. "You guys have outdone yourselves."

"*Thank* you," Mike said, throwing a towel over his shoulder. "Some people here," Mike paused, narrowing his eyes at Courtney and Tina, "have expressed doubts."

"Well, I have faith in this family," Mom said with a smile. "We make a great team."

"We do," Courtney said. As her eyes caught Tina's, a tiny, proud smile curled across Tina's mouth.

Rafi needed his diaper changed, so Mike took him upstairs while Courtney and Tina helped Mom straighten up the kitchen. They swept up crumbs from the burnt dinner rolls while Mom scooted around doing eight things at once. Watching her mother turn, wipe, and sort at full speed, Courtney felt a bit like she was watching a super-hero in her own kitchen.

When they all sat down for dinner, Mike raised his milk glass. "To teamwork," he toasted. Everyone clinked glasses with Rafi's sippy cup.

"How's the campaign stuff going, Maureen?" Tina asked, cutting into her pork chop.

Everyone looked surprised that Tina had asked.

"Hectic," Mom said. "Jackie's got a recycling event planned for Sunday." Mom ran a hand through her wavy hair. "I'm finally getting a haircut tomorrow. I wonder if

I should do something different with it."

"You should," Courtney said. "You've had the same hairstyle, like, forever."

"Thanks a lot," Mom said, pretending to be offended.

"Courtney's right," Tina added matter-of-factly. "It's time for a change."

"Okay," Mom relented. "One new hairdo coming up."

"Can Tina and I come?" Courtney asked.

"Of course," Mom said.

Tina shook her head, keeping her eyes on her plate. "I'll pass."

Courtney saw Mom and Mike exchange a look.

"Please?" Mom asked. "You're the hair expert in the family. I could really use your advice, Tina. Would you help me?"

Tina looked at Mom and hesitated. "Okay," she finally said. "If you need my help, I'll come."

Mother-Daughters Day

⚡ CHAPTER 10 ⚡

The next afternoon, Mom drove Courtney and Tina to the mall. Tina was quiet in the car. She was talking to Courtney again, but she wasn't exactly the fun Tina yet. Courtney was worried about how things would go.

The salon was on the mall's second level, a few doors down from Smiley's Arcade. A neon pink sign above the wide entrance spelled out "Radiance Salon" in cursive. The light reflected off the shiny black-and-white checked floor, giving the place a heavenly glow.

While they waited, Tina flipped through a hairstyle magazine. She gasped. "Look," she said, holding up a glossy picture of a woman with a thick mane of long curls, puffy bangs, and bubblegum-pink lipstick.

"Whoa," Courtney said. "She looks like Whitney Houston."

"Right?" Tina murmured in awe. "It's a spiral perm."

A tall woman with short platinum hair appeared. "Hi, Candice," Mom said.

"Maureen! It's so good to see you." The hairdresser

gave Mom a hug. "And you brought both girls! Come on back, everyone."

Courtney and Tina followed Mom past the reception desk to a brightly lit counter surrounded by mirrors. Mom sat down, and Candice wrapped a purple cape around Mom's neck. "What can I do for you today?" Candice asked.

Tina spoke before Mom could even open her mouth. "Frosted highlights and layers," Tina said confidently.

Raising an eyebrow, Candice met Mom's eye in the mirror.

"Tina is our family's hair expert," Mom said. "We're doing whatever she says."

Candice turned to Tina. "I've been trying to convince your mom to try highlights for years!" Candice patted Mom on the shoulder. "I'll go mix up the color." Then she disappeared into a back room.

Tina plopped down in one of the salon chairs. "You guys are so lucky to have curly hair," she said, opening the magazine she had been looking at.

"Really?" Courtney said. She had no idea Tina felt that way. "Why don't you just get a perm?"

Mom nodded. "I love your straight hair, Tina. But if you want to get a perm you may. I will pay for it."

Tina's head shot up. "Really?" she squealed. "That would be, like, amazing!"

Mom stood up. "I'll go see if one of the other stylists can do it today." She walked to the reception desk with her purple cape floating around her.

Tina was beaming. "Courtney, you should have something done, too."

Courtney squinted at herself in the mirror, wondering if Tina was trying to say her hair looked bad. "I don't need a haircut," Courtney said. "And I definitely don't need a perm."

Candice came out of the back room carrying a bowl of silvery-white, foul-smelling paste and a stack of foil squares. "You could get your ears pierced," she suggested to Courtney. "We just started offering it."

Courtney brightened. Sarah had gotten her ears pierced on her birthday last year, and now she wore tiny silver crescent moon earrings every day.

Mom came back from the front desk followed by a young woman with crimped red hair and several strands of long pearls. "Tina, this is Lindsey. She's going to do your perm."

"Awesome," Tina said. "Can Courtney get her ears pierced?" she asked as Lindsey waved her back to the shampoo bowls.

Mom laughed. "Why not? That way all the ladies in the family can have a salon treatment."

Candice began laying squares of foil under small sections of Mom's hair and dabbing paste on the sections with a paintbrush. Tina came back from her shampoo with wet hair and a cape around her shoulders. Lindsey combed Tina's hair and began rolling it in small rollers.

After Courtney picked out a pair of tiny gold stud earrings, she sat in a chair between Mom and Tina. A woman named Janice came to pierce Courtney's ears. She uncapped a red felt-tip pen and carefully drew a dot in the middle of each of Courtney's earlobes. Janice stood back and studied Courtney's ears. "That looks even," she said.

When Janice picked up a big metal tool that looked like a gun, Courtney felt her stomach tighten in a nervous twinge. "Is this going to hurt?" she asked.

"Only for, like, a second," Janice said.

"It's just a pinch," said Tina. She already had pierced ears. "You don't need to be scared."

As Janice took a step toward her, Courtney's hands flew up and covered both her ears. "Maybe I'll do this later," Courtney said.

"Hold my hand," Mom offered. "You can squeeze it as hard as you want."

"Hold my hand, too," Tina said on Courtney's other side. Mom and Tina each held out a cape-covered arm. Courtney took their hands. It steadied her, feeling their warm fingers around hers.

Janice carefully placed the piercing gun against Courtney's left earlobe. Courtney shut her eyes, gripping Tina's and Mom's hands harder. They squeezed back, and Courtney took another deep breath, wondering when it was going to—

THWACK! A quick, hot jab pummeled Courtney's ear.

"Whoa!" Courtney said. When she opened her eyes, there was a small gold stud in her left ear, where the red dot had been.

When Janice fitted Courtney's right earlobe into the piercing gun, Courtney kept her eyes open, but she still squeezed Tina's and Mom's hands again. She felt the hot pressure shoot into her earlobe.

"Done!" Janice announced. "That wasn't so bad, was it?" Courtney shook her head. Her earlobes were both bright red and throbbing, but on each one, a gold stud gleamed like a tiny prize.

Once Mom's hair was wrapped and Tina's hair was rolled, they both had to sit and "process." That meant wait. So Mom sent Courtney to Super Scoops for milk shakes. Back at the salon, the three of them sipped the creamy shakes and read magazines and sang along to the music playing on the salon's sound system.

"Talk about a fabulous mother-daughters day!" Candice commented when it was time to take the foils out of Mom's hair.

Courtney held her breath. Would Tina remind Candice that Maureen was not her real mom?

Instead, Tina softly said, "It is." Her perm solution still needed to set, so she sat in curlers while Courtney's mom got her hair cut into layers.

"Ta-da," Candice said after she dried Mom's hair.

"Wow, Mom," Courtney gushed. "You look amazing."

"You look like Princess Diana," Tina added.

Mom was beaming. "Thank you, Candice. And thank you, girls, for encouraging me. Tina, I couldn't have done this without you."

When Tina's perm was finally done processing, Lindsey took her back to the sink. They were there for another fifteen minutes before Tina returned to the chair. Her wet hair hung in tight curls.

As Lindsey dried it, Tina's hair transformed into a mound of soft spirals. "Oh my gosh," Courtney said when it was finished.

"It turned out nicely," Mom said admiringly. "What do you think, Tina?"

At first Tina didn't say anything. For a second, Courtney thought Tina hated it because she looked like she was going to cry. Finally she said, "I *love* it so much. Thank you, Maureen!" she said. "Thank you."

"You're welcome, sweetheart," Mom said. She gave Tina a squeeze and then headed up front to pay.

Tina glanced at Courtney. "What do you think?"

Tina actually cares what I think, Courtney realized. She paused for a moment, picking out the right words for exactly how she felt.

"I think we could pass for sisters," Courtney replied, and as they looked at each other in the mirror, Tina's face blossomed into a smile.

Door-to-Door

Jackie Barrett had become a regular fixture at Courtney's house, so Courtney wasn't surprised to see her in the kitchen with Mom the next morning. "What's happening today?" Courtney asked.

"It's your mom's first Curbside Chat," Jackie said, as though Courtney should know what that meant.

"That's what Jackie's calling our recycling event," Mom explained. "I'm going around the neighborhood to collect recycling. The goal is to show voters how a curbside pickup program would make it easy for all of us to recycle."

"We put flyers in people's mailboxes last week," Jackie said. "So hopefully folks have some recycling ready for your mom to collect."

"Oh yeah. Now I remember," Courtney said. "But Mom, if you're walking, what are you going to do with the cans and bottles and paper?"

"That's where I'm hoping you'll help," Mom said.

Jackie nodded. "While your mom chats, you can carry the stuff to my van. I've got boxes in the back so we can separate the recycling. Oh, and you can help hand out buttons, too." Jackie gestured to a box on the counter.

Courtney pulled out one of the blue and white pins from the box. It said "Maureen for Mayor." Courtney grinned. "Count me in."

◎

They started walking after lunch. Mom went up to each door while Courtney hung back, waiting to collect recycling.

"Hi there! I'm Maureen D'Amico," Mom would say to whoever answered the door. "I'm here to pick up your recycling and let you know I'm running for mayor."

Some people had forgotten about the recycling pickup, and some had no idea what Mom was talking about. Many not only had paper, glass, and aluminum ready, but were excited to talk to Mom about her ideas. Courtney offered everyone a button regardless of whether they had recycling.

Courtney and Mom had started on their own block, and Courtney knew everyone who came to the door. But as they kept walking, the faces became less familiar. Soon Courtney didn't know anyone. Mom knew a few people, but most were strangers. The farther they got from home, the more shy Courtney felt.

Mom, on the other hand, grew more and more confident as the afternoon went on. When people were willing to talk, Mom listened to their ideas and concerns. Courtney felt as if she were seeing a whole new Mom. *She's been transformed*, Courtney thought. *And it's not just her new hairdo.*

Not everyone wanted to talk about the election. One woman said, "I'm not interested in what you're selling," and closed the door before Mom said a word!

"It's always a mixed bag going door-to-door," Mom explained to Courtney. "Some people don't want to be bothered at home."

At a white house with green shutters, a ruddy-faced man narrowed his eyes over his glasses when Mom asked him if he had any recycling. "What do you want with my trash?" the man asked. When Mom tried to explain that she was running for mayor, the man started laughing. "A lady mayor who picks up my garbage. That's a good one."

The man started to turn away when Courtney offered him a button. "What does that say?" he asked, squinting at the blue and white button. "Maureen for Mayor? How about Maureen for Maid. You can clean the house!" He laughed again and slammed the door.

"That was . . . that was just . . . mean!" Courtney stammered. "Does he really think you should be a maid instead of a mayor?"

Mom sighed. "It's hard to believe, but some people still aren't used to women doing what men have always done."

"What are you going to do?" Courtney asked, still stinging from the man's laughter.

"Go to the next house," Mom said. "Knock on the next door. Keep going." Mom stepped off the porch.

Courtney followed Mom down the sidewalk, but her mind was in Crystal Starshooter's world. Crystal was wearing her space suit, going door-to-door to help the citizens of planet Trashtine escape from the piles of garbage that were threatening to make their planet uninhabitable.

"Is anyone in there?" Crystal called, pounding on the door of a white house with green shutters.

"Help," a weak voice called back. "I'm trapped. Help."

"Don't worry, sir," Crystal called back. "I'll help you." The door was locked, so Crystal had to break it down with a mighty kick. When the door burst open, stinky glass jars and dirty aluminum cans spilled out onto the porch.

"Over here," the voice called.

Crystal fought her way across the room to a man who was covered in recycling and trash. Only his head, glasses perched on his nose, appeared above the mess.

"I thought someone was here to rescue me," the man said. "You're just the maid."

"I'm not the maid. I'm Crystal Starshooter. I'm a space

explorer from the planet Earth."

Suddenly, an explosion rumbled outside and shook the house. Crystal almost lost her footing, but she fought to stay standing and not fall into the sea of garbage. "It's not safe here," Crystal cried. "I'll help you!"

"But space explorers are men," the man insisted. "You're a girl. You can't rescue me."

Another blast rocked the house, this time even harder. Crystal dug through the trash for the man's arm and tried to help him up. "We have to go. Now!" Crystal cried, but the man fought her off. "Sir!" Crystal shouted. "Sir?"

"Courtney?"

Courtney blinked. Mom was at the end of the sidewalk, waiting for her.

"Let's keep going, honey."

Courtney glanced back at the white house. "I'm right behind you, Mom," she said, running to catch up.

Countdown

Today's finally the day," Mr. Garcia announced as Courtney and her classmates filed into their room Tuesday morning. The other third-grade class joined them, and their teacher, Ms. Lee, wheeled in one of the school's televisions on a tall cart.

"This is so exciting!" Sarah bubbled as she pulled a chair between Courtney and Kip. Lively chatter filled the room as the teachers pulled the window shades and dimmed the lights so that everyone could see the image on the screen. "I hope nothing goes wrong this time," Sarah said. The launch had been delayed three times already.

"Remember, this is *live*," Mr. Garcia explained. "That means we're watching what's happening at Cape Canaveral, Florida, in real time."

Mr. Garcia turned up the volume. The commentator explained that the *Challenger* would be in orbit for six days and talked about the scheduled activities—including Mrs. McAuliffe's lessons from space. The screen showed images of the seven astronauts walking to the van that had carried them to the shuttle earlier that morning.

"There's Christa McAuliffe," Sarah said, as a woman with curly brown hair waved and smiled.

As she watched, Courtney thought again about how much Mrs. McAuliffe reminded her of Mom. Even though Mom's hair was different now, both women were doing something incredible.

"Don't you wish you were there?" Kip asked. Courtney and Sarah both nodded.

The launch was still a few minutes away, so kids talked and filled out the space-themed word search that Mr. Garcia had passed out. Finally, the countdown to liftoff began.

"In T-minus ten, nine, eight . . ." the announcer said.

"This is cool," Kip said in a hushed voice.

"Seven, six. We have main engine start. Four, three, two, one . . . and liftoff!" said the announcer, as the *Challenger* and its booster rockets rumbled off the ground, propelled upward by a thick column of orange-red flames.

"Liftoff of the twenty-fifth space shuttle mission, and it has cleared the tower!" continued the NASA announcer.

"Yay!" Sarah said, clapping her hands.

As the room filled with applause, Courtney kept her eyes glued to the screen. Her heart was thumping against her ribs as the *Challenger* cut across the deep blue sky, a plume of gray-white smoke trailing behind it.

Suddenly, a round cloud of dazzling white smoke burst into the sky, covering the *Challenger. Was that a booster rocket or something?* Courtney wondered. No one on TV said anything. Maybe this was a normal part of the launch.

Two plumes of smoke were now trailing out of the cloud ball where the *Challenger* had been, each plume falling in a different direction. But where was the *Challenger?* It had disappeared.

"What happened?" a voice said, and Courtney realized it was her own.

Kip shook his head. "I think it exploded."

"No, it didn't!" Sarah scolded him. "That's part of the liftoff ..." she trailed off, frowning at the white smoke on the TV screen.

"Was it a bomb?" Justin Wilson asked.

A flat voice on TV said, "Flight controllers here looking very carefully at the situation. Obviously a major malfunction."

Mr. Garcia crossed the room and switched off the TV. When he turned toward the class, his face was grim.

"We're not sure what's going on, so we're going to turn off the television for now."

Courtney couldn't stop staring at the dark TV screen. It was as if looking into the emptiness could help her understand what she had just seen—as if she could change the feeling in the pit of her stomach about what it meant. A moment ago she'd said she wanted to be at Cape Canaveral. Now she wanted to go home.

The next several minutes passed in a haze of worried glances and whispers. Principal Funk came in and took Mr. Garcia and Ms. Lee aside. As the adults talked in hushed tones by the classroom door, Courtney darted glances at her classmates. Some kids looked pale. Others, like Sarah, were struggling not to cry.

"Are the astronauts *dead*?" Sarah whispered.

Courtney couldn't bring herself to say out loud what

she was thinking. So she nodded, tears stinging her eyes.

Sarah started sobbing, and Courtney hugged her, trying not to look at the photos of Christa McAuliffe and the other *Challenger* astronauts on the wall. Mrs. McAuliffe was a teacher. And a mom. Mr. Garcia had said her family and some of her students were in Florida, watching the launch. Courtney felt sick, thinking about what they must be feeling. Courtney thought about her own mom. Where was she right now?

Ms. Lee called her class back to their room, and Principal Funk wheeled the television out. Mr. Garcia brought a stool up to the front of the room and sat down, facing Courtney and her classmates.

"Hey," he said quietly, with none of his usual playful pizzazz. "What you guys saw was pretty upsetting."

"Are the astronauts going to be okay?" Justin asked, his voice quavering.

Mr. Garcia took a deep breath. "I don't think so," he said. "It's likely that all seven astronauts were killed."

"Maybe you're wrong," Justin said. "Maybe something else happened—after you shut the TV off."

"I don't think so," Mr. Garcia said again.

Courtney's heart dropped. When she closed her eyes, she saw the puffy white cloud that had enveloped the space shuttle. The explosion hadn't looked like any explosion she'd ever seen in a movie or video game. The *Challenger* had just ... *disappeared*. It had vanished in silence at the exact moment that the white cloud of smoke had appeared, without any electronic bursts of noise like in a video game, or in a movie with a giant, earth-shattering *Ka-BOOM!*

Courtney glanced at the photo of the astronauts on the wall of the classroom. Now they were all dead—and she had watched it happen. If random bad things like this could happen to people like Christa McAuliffe and the other astronauts, then bad things could happen to anyone, anywhere, anytime.

"I'm scared," Courtney said.

Mr. Garcia nodded. "It's okay to be scared. It's also okay to be sad or confused or to not know how you feel."

Sarah sniffled, and he brought her a box of tissues.

"What do we do now?" Kip asked. "Will the space program ..." but his voice trailed off.

"Why did it happen?" Courtney asked.

Mr. Garcia looked at the floor for a long time. When he looked up again, there were tears in his eyes. "I don't know," he replied.

Aftermath

⚡ CHAPTER 13 ⚡

School got out early. When Courtney came out of the building, Mom was standing in the parking lot with several other parents. Courtney hurried to her, and Mom pulled her into a hug.

"Oh, sweetie," Mom whispered. "This is all so terrible."

Courtney felt empty. She didn't say anything. She just buried her face in Mom's jacket.

They drove to Tina's middle school. When they pulled up, Tina was sitting on the front steps. For once she wasn't surrounded by friends, talking a mile a minute. Courtney thought Tina looked younger somehow. As Tina walked to the car, Courtney could see that her stepsister's eyes were red from crying. Mom got out of the car and hugged her.

No one spoke on the drive home. Tina went upstairs and stayed there all afternoon. Courtney helped Mom make dinner. They talked about what Courtney had seen on TV. "Mom," Courtney admitted, "I always think of you when I see Christa McAuliffe. And today ..." Courtney started to cry. Mom wrapped her in a hug and they cried together.

Mike picked up Rafi from day care, and when they got home, Mike went up to see Tina. He was in her room for a long time and he came downstairs alone.

"Tina's not hungry," he said to answer the questioning look Mom gave him.

After dinner, Courtney wandered into the family room and turned on the TV. A news anchor appeared on-screen.

"President Reagan spoke to the nation's schoolchildren earlier," he said, "millions of whom were watching the live coverage of the shuttle's takeoff."

Courtney leaned forward, listening closely to the president's words. "I know it is hard to understand, but sometimes painful things like this happen," he said. "It's all part of the process of exploration and discovery. It's all part of taking a chance and expanding man's horizons. The future doesn't belong to the faint-hearted; it belongs to the brave. The *Challenger* crew was pulling us into the future, and we'll continue to follow them."

The phone rang, and Courtney switched off the TV. When she answered, it was her dad. Courtney almost started to cry again.

"I wanted to check on you," Dad said. "Your class watched the shuttle launch on TV, didn't it?"

Courtney told her dad about the morning and how school got out early. The two of them talked about the puff of white smoke and what happened to the astronauts. "We spent the last three weeks talking about them and their mission," Courtney said. "I sort of felt like I knew them. Especially Christa McAuliffe."

"I bet," Dad said. "I think a lot of students felt that way."

Courtney hesitated. "I was just watching the president on TV. He said that the future belongs to the brave. Do you think that's true?"

"I think it's hard to feel brave after something like this happens," Dad answered. "Doing something bold always carries a risk."

"Then why do it?" Courtney asked. "If it's safer not to take any risks, I mean?"

Courtney's dad hesitated. "Safer, yes. But some risks *are* worth it."

Courtney wondered how she would know if a risk was worth it. Suddenly, she felt terribly tired. "I'm glad you called, Dad."

"Me too, Court. I love you."

When Courtney went upstairs, the bedroom was dark, and she thought Tina was asleep. Courtney climbed up into the top bunk as quietly as she could. After a few moments, she heard a muffled sob from her stepsister's bed below her.

"Are you okay, Tina?" Courtney asked in the darkness.

"Not really," Tina whispered in a voice thick with emotion.

Courtney turned on the lamp that was clipped to the bed frame and scrambled down to the floor. Tina's face was wet with tears.

Courtney kneeled next to her bunk. "Are you upset about the astronauts?"

"Yes, but not just them," Tina replied, wiping her eyes. "When someone dies, it always makes me think of my mom."

Courtney looked at the photo of Tina's mom, Bonnie, that was always taped to the wall by Tina's pillow. Bonnie had the same long dark hair and wide smile as Tina.

"I miss her so much. My mom was really funny, did you know that?" Tina asked suddenly.

Courtney shook her head. She didn't know much about Tina's mom.

"She was. She liked to tell jokes and make people laugh," Tina continued. "She liked to dance, too. She made really good cupcakes. She braided my hair and she took me to the carousel at the zoo and she did special things with me all the time. Just like Maureen does with you. Sometimes I watch you and your mom together, and . . ." Tina gulped for air and then finished, "It hurts, because it reminds me so much of me and my mom."

"I didn't know that," Courtney said. Her heart ached for Tina. She wished there was something she could say to comfort her, but she knew there wasn't. Losing your mother was the most awful thing Courtney could imagine. She felt tears welling up in her eyes.

"I didn't tell you," Tina said quietly. She peeled the photo of her mother off the wall and held it in her lap. "When my mother got sick," Tina continued, "my parents told me there was a chance she might die, but it just didn't seem possible, you know? Even after it actually happened, it seemed *impossible*. Until Dad and Maureen got married. That's when I knew it was real. That my mom wasn't coming back."

Courtney's chest grew tight, and her tears spilled over.

"Sometimes when I see you and your mom together, it makes me angry and sad," Tina said, "because it reminds me all over again that my mother is gone."

Courtney swallowed. She missed her dad, but she could talk to him, just like she did tonight. He was still part of her life. Suddenly, Courtney could hardly breathe.

"It hurts so much," Tina continued. "Sometimes I just can't be around you and your mom."

"Is that why you didn't come watch Mom's TV interview?" Courtney said, thinking back.

Tina nodded.

"I wish you had said something," Courtney said softly.

"I didn't know how to talk about it," Tina admitted, tucking a curl behind her ear.

"What made you come to the salon with us?" Courtney asked.

"Because your mom asked. She said she needed me because I was the hair expert in the family," Tina said. "And I'm glad I went. It felt like . . ." she trailed off.

"Like we were a *family*," Courtney finished.

Tina nodded. She took a deep, shaky breath and looked Courtney in the eye. "I know that I've been mean to you. I am so sorry." She sniffed and blew her nose and then added, "I—I'm glad we're sisters."

A surge of love and understanding made Courtney's heart swell. "I am, too," she said, and before she knew it, they were hugging each other exactly the way sisters do.

A Lasting Impact

At school the next morning, the flag was at half staff. Students were quiet as they entered the building. In Courtney's classroom, the space posters and portraits of the astronauts were still on the walls.

Mr. Garcia sat on a stool in the front of the room and faced the class. "How is everyone doing?" he asked. For the next hour, the class talked about what they'd seen yesterday and how they felt. They talked about the president's speech, which lots of kids had watched.

"I was going to cancel your Dream Big presentations," Mr. Garcia said. "But when I heard the president's words last night, I realized that the best way to honor the *Challenger* crew is for us to keep going with the project. Are you with me on this?"

Courtney thought about her conversation with her dad and raised her hand. "I am," she said. "The astronauts were following their dreams. I think we should be brave and follow their example."

All around the classroom kids nodded in agreement. Mr. Garcia smiled.

"That's great, kids. I'm proud of you," he said. "We'll take the rest of this week to finish up our projects, and then we'll present them next week."

As Courtney's thoughts turned to her video game, however, uncertainty crept up inside her. She imagined Crystal Starshooter swinging from alien plant vines or defeating the evil princess. All that seemed very unimportant now. Courtney sighed.

"What's wrong?" Kip asked.

"My video game idea," she admitted. "It doesn't seem very good anymore."

"What are you *talking* about?" Kip replied, blinking at her in disbelief. "Your idea is great."

Courtney gave him a smile, but inside, she wasn't sure what to do.

That night after dinner, Courtney wandered into the family room, where Tina was watching television. But instead of MTV, the news was on.

Courtney sat down and listened to a report about a grade-school teacher who asked his students if any of them had had difficulty sleeping last night. All the kids raised their hands, and so did the teacher.

Courtney glanced at Tina. *We weren't the only ones who were awake last night,* Courtney thought.

On TV, a child psychiatrist was talking about how some kids might be reacting to the death of the astronauts, and especially Christa McAuliffe. "After their parents, teachers are, in most cases, the second most important adults in their lives," he explained. "Mrs. McAuliffe represented someone who is close to every child." Courtney felt tears sting her eyes.

Tina sniffled, and Courtney handed her a tissue. Courtney knew Tina was thinking of her own mom. Even though she felt sad, Courtney was glad she and Tina were together.

◎

For the rest of the week, Courtney worked on her video game presentation. By Saturday, she had all the levels represented on a display board, but she just couldn't decide how the game would end.

"Do you have any ideas?" she asked Parsley. Courtney was sitting on the beanbag chair in her room, her display board spread out in front of her. She was watching Parsley play with a Ping-Pong ball on the floor outside his cage.

Suddenly, Tina opened the door, and Parsley scurried across the room, right under Tina's bed.

"Parsley!" Courtney cried. She turned to Tina. "The cord to my lamp is under there. We have to get him out before he chews on it."

"I have an idea," Tina said, shutting the door quickly.

She grabbed a carrot stick from Parsley's food dish. Then she lay down on her stomach on the floor next to the bed. "Here, Parsley," Tina wheedled, waving the carrot under the bed.

Courtney was about to tell her it was useless when a small pink nose poked out from underneath the bed. Tina scooped Parsley into her hands, stood up, and watched him nibble the carrot stick.

Courtney was shocked. "Tina D'Amico, did you just pick up my guinea pig?"

Tina looked worried. "Did I do it wrong?"

"No," Courtney said. "But how did you learn that?"

"From watching you. You showed Rafi a million times."

"But you don't *like* Parsley."

Tina shrugged. "I'm getting used to him. I've never had a pet before. It's kinda fun."

"Wow," Courtney said. "So, wait, does this mean . . ."

"Yes," Tina said, nodding. "His cage can stay in our room. As long as you keep it clean."

Courtney caught her breath. "For real? He can stay?"

"Yes—but if he chews any of my scrunchies, he's toast," Tina said, putting Parsley back in his cage. She sat down next to Courtney and looked at the display board for her presentation. "How's all this going?"

"Not great," Courtney said. "I don't have an ending."

"I thought video games end when a player dies, and it's, like, 'Game Over'."

"Sure, when you *lose*," Courtney explained. "But some games have an ending when you get to the last level and *win*." Courtney couldn't believe they were actually talking about video games. Tina never played them.

"When I first started planning my game," Courtney continued, "I thought that at the end, Crystal Starshooter would win by blowing up the aliens and their planets and saving the Earth." Courtney thought about the *Challenger* and the puff of white smoke. "Now that all feels wrong."

"Why does she have to blow up the aliens?"

"Because they're the bad guys," Courtney said. "She has to defeat them."

"But . . . why?" Tina asked.

Courtney shrugged. "All video games are like that."

"Yours doesn't have to be," Tina insisted. "If you—"

"Wait," Courtney interrupted. "Say that again."

"Yours doesn't have to be," Tina repeated, confused.

"That's it!" Courtney shouted. "Tina, thank you! Now I know what to do!"

"What?" Tina asked.

"I'll show you as soon as I'm done," Courtney told Tina, giving her a sudden, grateful hug.

Crystal Starshooter's Universe

⚡ CHAPTER 15 ⚡

On Monday morning, Courtney had to take her display board to school, so Mom drove both girls to school before dropping off Rafi at day care.

As Courtney got out in front of her school, Tina reached out the window. "Here," she said, slipping her favorite bright pink scrunchie off her wrist and handing it to Courtney. "It's for good luck."

"Thanks," Courtney said, feeling a rush of affection for her stepsister.

"You'll be great, sweetie," Mom called as she drove away.

Courtney waved and then turned toward the school. Nervous energy was fizzing through her body. It was time to share Crystal Starshooter with her class.

◎

After taking attendance, Mr. Garcia snapped his rainbow suspenders with a grin. "Let's get this party started!"

The first name he called was Rachel Van Patten. She brought up a model of a car she had made and talked about her dream to build a solar-powered vehicle.

Next, Kip presented *A Film by Kip Tomatsu*. It was mostly

some neighbor kids dressed up like Ghostbusters running around trying to "capture" Kip's dog, Toby, who was wearing a rubber Halloween mask that looked like a ghost. It was pretty funny, especially when Toby shook off the rubber mask and started chewing it.

"That's going to be a blockbuster for sure!" Courtney whispered to Kip as he took his seat in front of her.

"I know!" he whispered back.

"Okay, next up," Mr. Garcia said. He closed his eyes and made a show of moving his finger down the class list. "Courtney," he crowed after he opened his eyes.

Courtney grabbed her display. Her heart was thumping as she set up her board, making sure everyone could see it. Then she fished a folded page of notes out of her pocket.

"This is Crystal Starshooter," Courtney began, gesturing at the drawing in the center of the board. Courtney had drawn Crystal holding her space helmet and gazing into the distance, her expression fearless. "Crystal Starshooter is the hero of my video game. She's a space explorer who travels the galaxy looking for alien tools that she can use to repair the Earth's ozone layer. The tools she finds will give her points and different superpowers."

As Courtney outlined some of Crystal's different tools, she noticed that the students were leaning forward at their desks. They seemed really interested.

"Each level of the game is a different planet, with a new alien enemy," Courtney explained. "On Level One, Crystal has to fight the big-collared aliens." Courtney stole a glance at Justin, whose polo shirt collar was standing straight up, as usual. "If you beat that level, then she moves up to Level Two to battle an evil, Hot Stick–throwing alien princess." Courtney pointed to her drawing of the princess, who still looked a lot like Tina.

"When you get to Level Three, Crystal repels a pair of alien twins with laser-shooting eyes using her ray blaster," Courtney said, pointing to her drawing of twins who bore a striking resemblance to the *Good Morning, Orange Valley!* anchors, Sandy Willen and Jefferson Caine.

"Then on Level Four, Crystal faces a garbage avalanche," Courtney continued, pointing out a drawing of Crystal knocking down the door of a white house with green shutters. "She's trying to rescue an alien who is trapped in a pile of trash and recycling, but the alien refuses her help." The alien looked a lot like the man who called Mom a maid when they went door-to-door collecting recycling and talking about curbside pickup.

"But on the final level, everything changes," Courtney said. "Because Crystal Starshooter discovers that in order to repair the Earth's ozone layer, she needs help from everyone—including the aliens."

"But I thought they were the enemies!" Justin Wilson called out, frowning.

"They *were* fighting each other, but it turns out that saving Earth is such a big job that Crystal needs everyone's help," Courtney explained. "So if you get to the end of Level Four, she gets an ancient alien bracelet that changes her powers. It reverses her ray blaster so that instead of defeating aliens, she can change them all into friends."

"So it's like a friend blaster," Sarah said. "That would be so cool—to turn all your enemies into your friends!"

"Exactly!" Courtney exclaimed. "Then once that's done, all the aliens use their combined powers to fix the hole in the ozone layer and save the Earth. Because even though Crystal Starshooter's a great explorer and she takes risks, she can't do it alone."

The room was quiet. Then the students began clapping.

"Good job," Mr. Garcia said as Courtney went back to her seat. "I like the game *and* the message."

"You should build it for real," Justin said. "It's a super cool idea."

"Yeah," Kip agreed as a few other kids nodded.

"Maybe someday," Courtney said thoughtfully.

"Although video games are just make-believe."

"With your imagination, I'm guessing you could make great things happen in the real world, too," said Mr. Garcia.

"Of course she will," said Sarah. "She's like her mom."

Courtney smiled with pleasure. Were Mr. Garcia and Sarah right about her? She had a good imagination, but was she really brave like her mother? Could she ever be heroic, like Crystal Starshooter?

There was only one way to find out: by doing real things, big things, important things. Even if there might be a risk in doing them, Courtney knew she would try.

Word List

You probably already know what these words mean, but did you know they were especially popular in the 1980s?

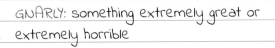

BOGUS: wrong or unfair

DUDE: a name you call someone to get their attention

DUH: a response to something that is obvious. You could answer someone's "duh" with NO DUH.

DWEEB: a nerdy person

GNARLY: something extremely great or extremely horrible

GRODY: disgusting

RAD: incredibly cool; a shortened version of "radical"

TOTALLY: used to emphasize the importance of something

TUBULAR: a term that surfers first used. It means great or awesome.

Courtney's World

When Ronald Reagan became president in 1981, lots of Americans were ready for a change. The 1970s had been a decade of challenges and conflicts. The Watergate scandal led to President Richard Nixon's resignation. America's involvement in the Vietnam War deeply divided the country. To many, President Reagan represented a brighter future for the United States. While not everyone agreed with his politics, the majority of Americans approved of his leadership. He made many people proud of their country and eager to move ahead.

A former Hollywood movie star, Reagan had a big smile and a friendly manner.

In the early 1980s, many Americans were struggling financially. Millions were out of work and in debt. As the decade progressed, more people found jobs and started spending money again. There were plenty of new toys, clothes, and electronics to buy. Americans were eager to have the newest

There were riots in some stores as shoppers fought for the most popular toy of 1983—the Cabbage Patch doll.

The Mall of America in Minnesota was the largest shopping center in the country when it opened in 1992. It had more than 5,000 stores and an amusement park.

and coolest products, especially items that were hard to get.

Shopping malls, like the Orange Valley Mall in Courtney's story, were built all over America. One of the most well-known malls was The Galleria in California's San Fernando Valley, which opened in 1980. It was the trendiest mall in the United States, and the teenage girls who hung out there were called *Valley Girls*. They were known for their obsession with shopping and for their habit of adding words such as "like" and "totally" to nearly every sentence.

Inside America's giant malls, shoppers could buy anything from clothes to toys to cassette tapes. They could grab a snack from dozens of restaurants in the food court or relax in seating areas to read the paper or people-watch. Video arcades and movie theaters were important parts of these malls—especially for kids like Courtney. Smartphones and social media didn't exist in the 1980s, so young people went to malls to see one another.

When they were at home, kids spent a lot of time in front of the TV. Cable networks such as CNN, HBO, and Nickelodeon began in the 1980s. By 1985, almost half of U.S. homes had cable. Videocassette recorders, or VCRs,

Video stores allowed people to rent movies and watch them at home—as long as the video they wanted was in stock.

changed the way people watched television. For the first time, viewers could record a network program and watch it whenever they wanted. By 1986, Americans had purchased 63 million VCRs.

Another massive change to Americans' television habits was the introduction of MTV. The network launched in 1981 and played music videos 24 hours a day. It was an instant hit. Music videos included everything from complex choreography to animation to special effects. The visual elements of the videos were as important as the music. Viewers loved seeing their favorite artists perform, and they began copying the dance moves, clothes, and hairstyles of music video stars, just like Courtney and Tina do.

Singers like Madonna became fashion icons.

In an era before the internet, most Americans learned of world events through television. For many children of the 1980s,

The Challenger *disaster was the first major tragedy to be broadcast on live television.*

one of the most memorable events was the *Challenger* space shuttle launch in January 1986. After President Reagan announced that he wanted a teacher to be the first civilian in space, more than 11,000 teachers applied. The winner was 37-year-old Christa McAuliffe, a high school teacher. Seeing an ordinary woman—a mother, wife, and teacher—preparing to go into space encouraged children to dream of new possibilities, and just like Courtney's class, they were deeply engaged in the *Challenger* launch.

Millions of schoolchildren watched the launch on television. They cheered and celebrated a successful liftoff.

Then, 73 seconds later, the space shuttle exploded. All seven crew members were killed. In classrooms all across America, kids struggled to make sense of what they had seen. Some teachers turned off the television, and some prayed. Some children cried, and some sat in

Those who witnessed the space shuttle launch in Florida reacted with shock, disbelief, and grief.

silence. Instead of a triumphant moment in history, they'd witnessed one of the nation's greatest tragedies.

That evening, President Reagan appeared on television to talk about the *Challenger.* He spoke directly to America's schoolchildren and told them not to give up on their dreams or on the country's dream of space exploration. Many children followed his advice, and NASA received thousands of letters from children asking the agency to continue the space program. Even when many adults thought space exploration

Students created sympathy cards for families of the Challenger *crew.*

was too dangerous, kids, inspired by Christa McAuliffe and the *Challenger* crew, continued to dream big.

Christa McAuliffe's story was especially personal to Courtney because her own mom was trying to break boundaries by running for mayor. The 1980s saw more women joining the workforce and taking on roles that had previously been held by men. While opportunities were expanding, women still earned less money than men, even when they did the same job. Working moms faced additional challenges because many employers assumed they couldn't care for their children and be committed to their work. Courtney's mom experienced that sort of prejudice when she was running for mayor.

Working women learned to use new computer technology.

Family life in the 1980s looked different from that of previous generations. Many families needed two incomes to make ends meet. With both parents working, school-age kids, like Courtney and Tina, often spent some time alone during the day. Some of those kids were growing up in single-parent families. From 1960 to 1980, the nation's divorce rate more than doubled. Divorce was a common experience for many families, and Ronald Reagan was the first divorced president in U.S. history. Throughout the 1980s, the stigma of divorce was increasingly replaced by social acceptance. Today, many different types of families are recognized and celebrated.

The trends and new technologies of Courtney's time shaped the way we live today. The personal computers and cordless phones of the 1980s became the laptops and smartphones we use today. The women who took on male-dominated roles in the workforce paved the way for greater gender equality for girls and women.

Recycling, which was important to Courtney and her mom, grew in popularity in the 1980s and 1990s.

BOOK TWO

Courtney's Story Continues

Courtney's having an awesome summer with her friends! She and Sarah have sleepovers almost every night. They go to the mall with Kip, ride bikes, watch movies, and swim in Courtney's pool. But the arcade is still Courtney's favorite place to be. That's where she meets Isaac. He's even better at video games than Courtney. She tells him about her made-up hero, Crystal Starshooter, and Isaac has gnarly ideas to add to Courtney's game world. The two become good friends, and Isaac starts hanging out with Kip and Sarah, too. When an issue with Isaac comes between Courtney and Sarah, Courtney doesn't know what to do. Can she support her new friend without losing her best friend?

READ MORE ABOUT THESE
AMERICAN GIRL CHARACTERS
AT BOOKSTORES AND AT AmericanGirl.com:

a Nez Perce girl who
loves daring adventures
on horseback

a Hispanic girl
growing up on a rancho
in New Mexico

who is determined
to be free in the midst
of the Civil War

a Jewish girl with
a secret ambition to
be an actress

who faces the
Great Depression with
determination and grit

who joins the
war effort when Hawaii
is attacked

whose big ideas get
her into trouble—but
also save the day

who finds the
strength to lift her voice
for those who can't

who fights for the
right to play on the
boys' basketball team

OCT - - 2020